Ibiza
Summer

Anna-Louise Weatherley was born in Southampton and grew up in London where she still lives. An award-winning writer for over ten years, she is the former editor and acting editor of *J-17* and *Smash Hits* respectively and has written for magazines including *New Woman*, *Company*, *Arena*, *Grazia* and *More*. This is her first novel. When she is not writing, Anna-Louise collects vintage bikinis – at the last count she owned over a hundred.

Also available by Anna-Louise Weatherley:
The Wrong Boy

Ibiza Summer

Anna-Louise Weatherley

Piccadilly Press • London

For Joe and Pat –
a love story that stood the test of time.

Huge thanks to Brenda Gardner, Melissa Patey,
Yasemin Uçar and everyone at Piccadilly,
everyone at CosmoGIRL! and to Alan and Louie,
my two favourite boys in the entire world.

First published in Great Britain in 2006
by Piccadilly Press Ltd,
5 Castle Road, London NW1 8PR
www.piccadillypress.co.uk

This edition published 2010
Text copyright © Anna-Louise Weatherley, 2006

A catalogue record for this book is available
from the British Library

ISBN: 978 1 84812 129 4 (paperback)

1 3 5 7 9 10 8 6 4 2

Printed in the UK by CPI Bookmarque Ltd, Croydon, CR0 4TD
Cover design by Simon Davis
Cover illustrations by Sue Hellard

Mixed Sources
Product group from well-managed
forests and other controlled sources
www.fsc.org Cert no. TT-COC-002227
© 1996 Forest Stewardship Council
FSC

Chapter 1

'The red, oh yeah, *definitely* the red. What do you reckon, Ellie?' Narinda was holding one of Ellie's favourite dresses up against me for size, her head cocked to one side thoughtfully. For a nanosecond I dared entertain the idea that she might let me borrow it, but I wasn't holding out much hope. Ellie referred to this particular dress as her 'IT' dress and would almost certainly want to wear it herself, what with tonight being special and all. Besides, I'd been coveting it for months back home and she'd never even let me so much as look at it, let alone try it on. The fact that she wasn't already throwing a fit suggested she was only playing ball so as not to look like a right mean cow in front of her mates.

'OK, *OK*,' Ellie sighed as she began to towel dry her hair. 'You can wear it on one condition: don't go within ten feet of anyone holding a cigarette and don't even *think* about jumping in the pool in it – no matter what anyone else might be seen doing – got it?'

'That's two conditions,' Narinda pointed out helpfully.

'Hey, whose flippin' side are you on?' Ellie snapped back, unable to stifle a grin.

I squealed with delight and ran over to hug my sister, who was still a bit damp from the shower she'd just taken.

'You're the best!' I said and meant it because I knew

that in the grand scheme of things, as far as fulfilling the 'cooler older sister' role goes, Ellie had surpassed herself already by bringing me on her annual girls' holiday with her equally cool girlfriends – and now it looked like she might lend me her favourite dress to boot. It was all sounding a bit too good to be true.

'Try it on then!' ordered Narinda impatiently. 'Let's see what it looks like before you agree to all the terms and conditions!'

I liked Narinda. She was Ellie's best friend and they had, along with Charlotte and Louisa, met while they were at secondary school together, forming a formidable 'girl gang' that had stood the test of time. Like everyone associated with my sister, Narinda was incredibly beautiful, with long, impossibly glossy black hair and almond-shaped brown eyes that set off her coffee-coloured skin perfectly. She looked like an exotic Indian princess and was nice too; funny, if a bit bonkers at times. I could tell she was making an effort with me and I was genuinely grateful, because she didn't have to or anything, especially since this was supposed to be a holiday for her and her mates and the last thing she probably wanted was to chaperone her mate's little sister who didn't have any decent clothes to wear.

'Give it here,' Ellie said, tugging at the dress as I struggled to do up the zip. 'There you go.'

I stood, slightly awkwardly, in front of the mirror and my heart sank. It was official: Ellie's 'IT' dress, which made *her* look like a supermodel, hugging all the right places and giving her a cleavage to die for, made *me* look like a bag lady. The feather-soft chiffon fabric pulled and puckered at my hips, making it appear as if I had a big pair of granny knickers on underneath, and somehow it managed to make my curvy belly stick out even more than usual. In short, it was a disaster.

'See, it looks fantastic!' said Narinda, a little too brightly to be convincing.

'Yeah, you look pretty,' said Charlotte, adding, 'honestly,' even though I'd not said anything to suggest I didn't believe her.

Ellie was the only one who was sort of truthful.

'Hmm. Not sure if it's you, Iz.' She said it as light-heartedly as possible so as not to send me sobbing into the bathroom, which is exactly what I felt like doing.

With the show over, Louisa went back to straightening Charlotte's hair and turned the stereo up. Ironically, it was playing 'Dress You Up' by Leanne, which was proving to be the club hit of the summer.

I bet Leanne doesn't have this kind of problem, I thought to myself as Narinda began frantically pulling at the fabric around my hips in some vain attempt to make the dress fit better.

'I look like I'm pregnant,' I said, my voice cracking slightly as I rushed to take it off.

Louisa laughed and Ellie shot her a look as if to say shut up.

'Well, thanks anyway,' I said, handing the dress back to Ellie and feeling utterly crushed. 'You wear it; it looks much better on you.'

'Look, there's some other stuff in my case,' Ellie said softly. 'Have a rummage; there'll be something else.'

I knew that no matter what I tried on of Ellie's I'd never look as good in it as she would. When it came to claiming killer figures, my elder sister must've caught the early bus and got the pick of the rack, while somehow I must've missed three in a row and got there just in time to pick up the dregs no one else wanted from the bargain bin. According to Mum, I'd inherited her side of the family's shape while Ellie had lucked out and got our dad's side. Mum called it the 'Francis's Roundness' – all hips and no bust. And then there was the whole hair business too. When I'd demanded to know who was responsible for my unruly mass of long, dark-brown curls, Mum had replied that she had no idea because everyone had straight hair on both sides of our family, aside from my Auntie Maureen, whose hair was slightly wavy (although Mum wasn't sure if this was due to having had a bad perm back in the Sixties). 'It must be a throwback from somewhere down the line, a latent gene,' she'd decided, which as you can imagine didn't exactly make me feel a whole lot better.

I looked down at my suitcase and wondered if I'd remembered to bring my trusty old black halter-neck top and if I could get away with teaming it with my denim skirt. Would that be dressy enough? I didn't have a clue, because when I actually thought about it I realised I'd never been to a proper pool party before.

I emptied my case out on the floor in frustration and looked at all the clothes I'd spent so much time and effort carefully choosing to bring with me, which now looked really tacky and crap and inappropriate for a glamorous and cool pool party.

'So, d'you reckon Drogo will be there tonight?' Charlotte asked no one in particular as Louisa continued to straighten her hair. 'I think he's cute.'

'Charlie, Charlie, Charlie,' said Ellie wearily with a warning tone in her voice that I was familiar with. 'The man's a player. You saw what he was like last year – after anything in a skirt . . .'

'And trousers or shorts . . .' added Narinda, giggling.

'Still, Drogo or no Drogo,' said Louisa, 'it's bound to be another night to remember, full of the most gorgeous Ibizan totty all waiting to be knocked sideways by our scintillating conversation and wowed by our ample charms!' She grabbed her boobs and squished them together to accentuate her cleavage, and everyone laughed.

'Yeah, it's about bloody time we spent an evening talking to some exciting blokes for a change, eh, Ellie?' said Charlotte, putting her tongue firmly in her cheek and winking at the others. Ellie was wise to Charlotte's teasing though.

'I'm just window-shopping tonight, ladies – looking but not buying.'

I knew that Ellie would never cheat on her boyfriend, Tom. They were far too much in love, although I couldn't help but wonder how he felt about his beautiful girlfriend being on holiday with her almost-as-equally beautiful and very single mates. I wanted to say something to Charlotte, like how I knew that Tom and my sister were made for each other because I could see it in their eyes whenever they were together, but I thought it best to keep schtum as I wasn't quite sure if I was allowed to join in or not.

From what I could gather from the conversation, Alfredo was somewhat of a face on Ibiza's infamous party circuit and in the four years that Ellie and her gang had been coming here they'd never missed one of his show-stopping parties.

Great, I thought. I was about to go to what was fast sounding like the event of the century and I had *nothing* to wear. I knew that if Willow were here with me she'd have it sorted in seconds and make me feel better about the whole red dress episode earlier. I sighed. It had only been forty-eight hours and I missed her so much already.

I was last in the bathroom as I figured that was my place, and I would've only felt pressurised to get ready really quickly if one of the others had been waiting to go in after me so I didn't really mind. I decided to do my make-up first and then tackle the whole hair-straightening business last, even though I knew that however much I attempted to iron out my curls, a few hours later it would revert back to looking like I'd stuck my finger in a plug socket and flicked the switch. I put on some mascara and applied an extra coat of my new watermelon-flavoured lip-gloss, my skin tingling from the warm shower and from the day's sun. I spritzed my hair with serum, although I didn't know why I was bothering. What I needed was a product specially made for me – 'Anti Iz-Frizz' or something. I sighed again and rubbed a little pink glitter over my eyelids and a sprinkling on my shoulders – not too much because I didn't want to resemble 'a tart lit up like a Christmas tree', as Greg, Mum's boyfriend, had so delightfully suggested one night as I was on my way out to meet Willow.

I was annoyed with myself for not feeling more excited about the pool party. Instead of feeling like the luckiest girl on the planet, which according to everyone else I was, I felt nervous and anxious. Would I stick out like a sore thumb? Who would I talk to and what would I say? Would I look stupid dancing and would everyone be watching me?

I wasn't sure why I was so worried. I mean, it wasn't like I'd never been to a party before.

'Get a grip, Isabelle,' I said aloud. 'Isn't this the kind of thing you've been waiting for? Hanging out with a cooler, older crowd?'

My thoughts were broken by a sudden knock at the door.

'Only me, Iz,' said Ellie in a sing-song voice. 'Wow, your make-up looks fab,' she said, sounding surprised, as I let her in. She was holding what looked like a dress in one hand and belt in the other.

'It does?' I said, trying not to sound too chuffed and failing.

'Look, I reckon I've found you something to wear.' She placed the dress and belt into my hands. I could tell she felt bad about what had happened earlier and I suddenly realised how sensitive my sister could be.

'Oh, you don't have to . . .'

'Shut up, Izzy, and try it on,' she said, rolling her eyes.

'OK, but I'd rather do it alone this time, if you don't mind.'

Ellie turned to walk out of the bathroom.

'Els . . .' I suddenly found myself saying.

'*Yeeeess?*'

'Can I ask you something?'

'No, you can't borrow my new sandals as well.'

'No, not that,' I said, lowering my eyes uncomfortably. 'I was just wondering about tonight . . .'

'What about it?'

'Well – will I, you know . . . Do you think I will . . . ?'

I really didn't want Ellie to know I felt awkward and worried about tonight. I wanted to come across as confident and outgoing, someone she could hang out with and have a laugh with – a friend – but my nerves really had started to get the better of me.

'Don't be daft,' she said, totally pre-empting what I was going to ask. 'You're going to look fab and we'll all be there to —'

I knew she was about to say 'look after you', but she stopped short of actually saying it. 'Anyway, it'll be fun and I promise not to cramp your style,' she mocked. 'Now hurry up and get dressed,' she said, her usual bossy tone reinstated. 'You're holding us up.'

She closed the door behind her and I began to inspect the little black dress. It had tiny puffed sleeves and a low neckline that I hoped was just low enough for it not to be too embarrassing. I'd admired it on Ellie on many occasions and would've settled for looking just half as fabulous in it as she had. I slipped it on over my head and let it slide down my body. The dress hugged my waist perfectly and then flared out from the hips a little. It was quite short, shorter than anything I usually wore, but it felt good. *Really* good. I took the belt, which was leather with a big brass round buckle, and wrapped it round my waist as I stood back from the mirror and examined myself. I looked different, but I wasn't sure how exactly. Glamorous? Sexy, even? Looking back at myself in the mirror I felt a sudden burst of confidence. The dress gave me an older, more glamorous vibe, like I might actually belong in Ellie's effortlessly cool girl gang. I checked my bra straps weren't on show and cheekily spritzed myself all over with Louisa's big bottle of Angel perfume, which she'd left on top of the basin. I took a final deep breath. Perhaps tonight wasn't going to be so bad after all.

Chapter 2

Alfredo's villa was set back among a sea of lush olive groves, high up on the cliffs, causing the clapped-out old banger of a taxi we were all squashed in to pop and groan and heave up the steep hill.

'Are we almost there yet?' I asked hopefully, my bum all but gone to sleep.

'Not long now,' said Charlotte, pointing to the imposing white house in the near distance. 'Beautiful, isn't it? Just wait until you get inside.'

My heart was beating so fast in my chest I swore if the car hadn't been making such a racket, Ellie, whose lap I was sitting on, would've heard it. It was all beginning to sink in fast. I was really here, in Ibiza, in the back of a cab with my sister and her cool friends, just about to go to a private pool party. It was all a bit surreal, especially since this time last week Willow and I had been chilling out at her place watching *From Here to Eternity*, courtesy of her dad's old black-and-white film collection, and talking about how nothing much exciting ever happens to us.

How things change in a week, I thought. But then I knew that already, what with my dad and the whole 'Toby scenario'. Even though I'd promised myself I wasn't going to think about Toby Parker, I found my thoughts sub-consciously, and somewhat annoyingly, drifting in his direction.

* * *

Toby and I had got together on the fifteenth of March, the night of Sarah Ferris's birthday. We'd been together for less than two and a half months which, by my standards, was nothing short of a marriage, when he unceremoniously and suddenly broke it off. His dumping text message had read: IZ. AM SO SOZ BUT ITS NOT WRKING OUT BTWEEN US. STILL WANT 2 B M8S BUT FINK WE SHLD CALL IT A DAY.

'What an absolute tosser,' Willow had said furiously when I had shown her the text and although I tried not to let her see how bothered I was, she knew that secretly I was gutted. What was even more galling was that Toby had been the one to do all the chasing at first.

Toby played football for a local team and had huge hazelnut eyes and long eyelashes, but when all was said and done I wasn't *that* bothered about him. It wasn't until we started talking properly that he began to grow on me – 'like fungus' as Willow had later put it.

Willow, on the other hand, had fancied Toby's mate, Joe Jenkins, for what seemed like a lifetime. Joe had a bit of a reputation for being a bad boy. He drank too much beer and got into fights for no reason. Not only that, Willow was different when she was around him, although I couldn't put my finger on how exactly. Their relationship was more off and on than a light switch, and I'd never met a couple who checked up on each other as much as they did. At that time, they were indefinitely off, due to the fact that Willow had discovered Joe had been secretly texting another girl. Wils never knew where she stood with Joe – a situation which would've driven me nuts – and as a result she was always stressed out about him. For me, relationships were all about trust. Going out with someone meant finding a soulmate; having a laugh and chilling out together, being friends and sharing things, not worrying yourself sick that they might go off with someone else as soon as your back is turned.

I could tell Toby had plucked up a lot of courage to ask me out, because he'd stammered his way through it and looked all hot and uncomfortable, which I thought was sweet and made me feel a bit sorry for him. It was a standard date; we went to the cinema followed by pizza. We'd talked about football and he told me his dream was to play for Manchester United one day. I knew he was supposed to be a pretty good footballer by all accounts, so I told him he should follow his heart and not let anything or anyone stand in the way of his dream, and he'd looked at me a bit strangely after I'd said it. I sensed he was different from any of the other lads I'd been out with before (total: three). He wasn't a beer monster like a lot of Joe Jenkins's posse were, he seemed more mature than that.

That night, after the pizza, he'd kissed me and although fireworks hadn't exactly gone off, it was still kind of nice. Willow was ecstatic that I'd managed to find a boyfriend who Joe was mates with as it meant we could do the whole double date thing, and the next few times we went out it was the four of us, which was cool.

So it was just when I'd decided I wanted to really make a go of things with Toby that the text came. Looking back, maybe he'd been a bit quieter than usual on our last date.

But he had asked me about my dad as he knew it was approaching the anniversary of his death all those years ago, and I'd been so touched that he'd remembered that I wanted to hold him and not let go. So I was doubly shocked and hurt. Not to mention embarrassed. Being dumped by text is just the worst thing ever, as basically it meant he didn't even like me enough to phone me, let alone tell me to my face. That wasn't the worst of it, though. A week or so later, I'd found out that Janie Phillips from Year Ten had gone to watch him play football at some county championship match and that they were now seeing each other. This wouldn't have been so bad had she not been stunning and, just sixteen, almost a whole year younger than me.

I had hoped Toby might be different. He had seemed sensitive and caring when he had asked me about my dad and then suddenly, with no explanation, it was all over.

'What do you expect?' Willow had said. 'He's a boy!'

Maybe my expectations *had* been too high. I wanted romance; deep and meaningful conversations, putting the world to rights over endless cups of cappuccino as we gazed longingly into each other's eyes; I wanted friendship and trust.

I suppose I couldn't entirely blame Toby. I couldn't even find my voice around him half the time. Whenever I met anyone I fancied, I'd find myself tongue-tied and unable to speak coherently. In the unlikely event that something *did* manage to pass my lips, I felt sure it was never that interesting and always sounded so stilted and unnatural.

Still, it seemed to me that whenever you started liking a lad back, that's precisely the time you got dumped, so I decided I didn't want to take any more chances. I was steering clear of boys until I felt sure I wouldn't have my heart broken.

'*Ya estamos quí,*' said the taxi driver, snapping me back to reality.

'*Gracias,*' said Ellie, and we watched as he pulled away back down towards the road. This was it. We had arrived.

I inhaled deeply and tried to erase my memory of Toby Parker. He could go jump in a lake for all I cared now. It was time to leave the past behind and have some fun.

Chapter 3

The air smelled sweet and there was a gentle warm breeze blowing. Outside the door to the imposing house, illuminated by a small night-light, was a white tiled sign that read, *Villa Paraíso*, and I was aware of the sound of loud music thumping in the distance.

We hadn't even rung the bell before it swung open and a tall thick-set man dressed in a white linen shirt with no collar and designer-looking jeans stood with his arms outstretched. I noticed he wasn't wearing any shoes.

'*Hola*, Ellie . . . *y* Rinda,' he said loudly, kissing my sister and embracing Narinda simultaneously. 'Lotte, Lotte . . . *y* Louisa. *Me alegro de volver a verte* . . . *¡Cuánto tiempo sin vernos!* An ooh is zis?' he asked, pointing directly at me. I felt my face burn.

'This is Izzy, my sister. Izzy this is Alfredo,' Ellie said, pulling me in closer to her like a wayward toddler. I held out my hand for him to shake it, but he grabbed me with full force and kissed me on both cheeks, his dark stubble scratching my face.

'Izzy. *¡Bienvenida!* I am pleeeesed to meeeeet you . . . Beautiful, beautiful . . . *¡Pasa! Adelante* . . . come in, come in . . .'

Inside, the atmosphere hit me immediately. Everywhere around us people were laughing and chatting as dance music and thick cigarette smoke pumped through the air. 'C'mon,' said Ellie, grabbing my hand excitedly, 'let's go outside to the pool and get a drink.' I held on to her hand tightly as we fought our way through the throng of people, tanned naked limbs making a thousand shapes around us.

'Look at her!' screamed Narinda, pointing excitedly to a girl who was wearing an elegant white dress which was almost see-through. On one arm she must've had at least fifty small gold bangles and I noticed her belt was in the shape of a snake and her matching gold sandals were laced up high to her knee – she looked like Cleopatra.

Guys were standing around drinking and chatting to girls or to each other, their bronzed chests on display or covered in loose white shirts or T-shirts and three-quarter length trousers or jeans, which seemed to be the uniform.

Outside appeared even bigger than inside and was just as lively, with a huge sunken swimming pool taking centre stage and a bar at the back surrounded by palm trees, where people were drinking from large glasses decorated with pineapples and little sparklers. Stripy blue sun loungers cascaded around the edges of the pool and groups of girls and boys and kissing couples were draped over them decadently. I had to remember to text Willow, take some pictures on my phone and send them to her. She would have a fit if she could see this!

'Oh my God, there's Lorna from last year!' screamed Ellie, pointing in the direction of a small dark-haired girl. 'Let's go and say hello.'

'We'll be back in a bit.' Narinda turned to me and smiled apologetically as Ellie dragged her off. I watched them as they went over, the dark-haired girl shrieking with delight when she caught sight of my sister. Would I ever be as popular as Ellie? I wondered as I watched more and more people greet my sister with huge hugs and kisses. Ellie seemed to have a way about her that made people feel happy and at ease, and I wanted people to feel that way about me too. She was funny and pretty and smart, having got a 2:1 in her English language degree before going on to study law, and people admired her, not just for her looks but for her personality too.

Despite the six-year age gap, there had been a time when Ellie and I had been close, although these days she was always busy with her studies, with friends, with work, with Tom . . . and as a result we saw less and less of each other. Mostly though, I wished I could talk to her about dad, but the few times I had plucked up enough courage to try, she had always swiftly changed the subject or said, 'Not now, Izzy,' like I'd annoyed her. She didn't want to talk to me about it and that was that. So once again, I was left with all these emotions that had nowhere to go – they just stayed there, swimming around my head like goldfish trapped in a bowl.

I leaned back against a palm tree and closed my eyes for a second. I had to try not to think too much. I wanted to enjoy the moment. *Think happy thoughts, Iz, happy thoughts.*

I was watching everyone dancing and chatting and

laughing from a distance, gearing myself up to maybe go and start a conversation with someone and help take my mind off things, when Ellie suddenly remembered I existed and beckoned me over to meet her friends. There was Lorna, twenty-three from Oxford, who they'd met at Alfredo's party two years ago, and her friends, Kaz, Leigh and Rebecca, also twenty-three, who all seemed really friendly and as excited to be there as I was.

Ellie explained that this was my first time in Ibiza, which caused much oohing and ahhing as they all scrabbled to tell me about all the fabulous places I should see and what clubs to go to and which ones to avoid. Rebecca asked me which uni I went to, which made me feel pretty good as obviously she must've thought I was older, and seemed surprised when Ellie annoyingly butted in and told her I was still at secondary school, albeit on my way to Sixth Form. I would have told the truth anyway and felt irked that Ellie had felt so compelled to interject.

We all chatted for a while and I began to feel a bit more relaxed, although I was conscious of what I was saying and chose to ask a lot of questions so as to avoid having to answer any myself.

Eventually everyone began to tail off and move on to other people and conversations and I was left on my own again, not that I minded too much as by now my head was buzzing with names and words and places and I was a bit overawed by it all – besides, I needed the loo.

I made my way through the maze of people in the main room and up the winding staircase, which was littered with bodies. I was pretty desperate for a wee by now, but with so many people and so many bedrooms and doors to open, I realised I would have to bite the bullet and ask someone.

'Are you lost?' a voice from behind me said, and I spun round.

'Do I look lost?' I replied, realising immediately that this could've sounded a bit defensive, even though I hadn't meant it like that.

'Yeah, you do a bit,' he said, smiling.

I was immediately struck by his eyes. Emerald green. That was the only way I could describe them. They were bright and piercing and they seemed to be looking deep inside me, which made me feel uncomfortable and excited at the same time. 'If you're looking for the loo, it's just through here,' he said, pointing to his left and clearly reading my mind. 'Shall I show you?'

'No, no!' I said a little too quickly. 'It's fine, no problem. I'll find it.'

'Cool,' he said, still smiling as he walked away, and I couldn't help but notice what a beautiful smile he had.

Back downstairs the party was kicking off harder than before, with even more people dancing and cheering and throwing shapes to the constant boom, boom, bass of the beats. I looked around to see if I could spot Ellie and Co., but they were nowhere to be seen. I reckoned they were probably outside so decided to brave the ravers in the main room and go and find them.

I'd almost made it to the door when I heard a voice over the microphone say, 'Hey, the girl in the black dress – you!' I turned round to look, but couldn't see anyone and didn't think they would be talking about me anyway; it wasn't as if I was the only girl wearing a black dress.

'Hey! Toilet girl!'

I froze. Oh. My. God. Was someone talking to me?

I looked over the crowd and clocked the guy with the green eyes who'd directed me to the loo. He was standing up on the DJ booth waving his hands at me and smiling that lovely smile . . . I wasn't sure what to do, so I half-heartedly waved back at him, feeling like a total chump.

'I hope you found the bathroom to your liking!' he shouted over the mike at me and people began to giggle and stare.

I wanted to turn and run but I was rooted to the floor and each time I went to move my legs it felt as though I was treading water in a bucket of treacle.

Toilet girl! How embarrassing is that? I thought as I finally managed to make my way outside. I wasn't sure which way I was going as it was dark by now and somehow I must've made a wrong turn – I ended up round what seemed like the back of the villa and on to a small patio area. There were huge beanbags strewn everywhere with people sitting in them, chatting and laughing. It was quieter and the music was softer, more ambient than in the rest of the villa. There was a gentle glow coming from the candle lanterns that were randomly scattered around and I could hear the sound of crickets in the grass, reminding me that it was summer and I was on holiday and should be happy.

I noticed a group of people leaning over the edge of the patio, looking out to the distance. They sounded excited about something and I was intrigued to know what, so, having spotted a space far enough away from them so it didn't look like I was trying to gatecrash their moment, I went over to take a look.

'Wow!' I gasped involuntarily. Below me and stretched out for what looked like miles were hundreds of tiny lights igniting the dark night like little sparkly glow-worms. I could just about see the shoreline in the distance as the light from the town below caught the sea's reflections, making the waves twinkle and shine like it had been scattered with a thousand diamonds. I guessed it must be Ibiza Town and I wondered if there was anyone down there looking up at me looking down at them.

'I think you dropped something,' a voice behind me said quietly, although it still made me jump.

Flippin' heck. It was the green-eyed guy from before.

I turned round and, to my horror, I saw that I'd left a trail of stuff in my wake: my lip-gloss, comb, money, phone, old tissues, my little photo wallet and a half-eaten packet of cherry drops were strewn across the floor behind me. My bag must've broken. Embarrassed, I bent down on my hands and knees and frantically began scrabbling on the ground to retrieve it all.

He knelt down in front of me and did the same.

'Think your bag may have sprung a leak,' he said, smiling as he handed me some loose coins and my photo wallet. His skin touched mine, only fleetingly and so lightly it felt like a whisper, but it was enough to stiffen my spine and cause my skin to prickle all over.

'Yes,' I agreed, feeling myself blush. I looked at my bag and saw that the bottom stitching had all but come apart.

'I'm sure you can get it mended,' he said reassuringly as I stuffed the remains of the contents back in and turned it upside down to prevent a similar occurrence.

I felt so self-conscious that I was afraid to speak and when I tried, a horrible husky noise came from me that sounded almost animal-like. I cleared my throat.

'Yes . . . hope so,' I finally managed to say.

Although I couldn't properly look at him, I knew he was gorgeous, I could *feel* it. I felt intimidated and shy, not to mention painfully embarrassed by the whole 'toilet girl' thing earlier.

He held out his hand and gestured for me to give him the bag so that he could inspect the damage. But my hands were paralysed and I could only stare.

'Really, it's fine. It's vintage,' I said, because it sounded posher than saying 'it's old'. 'It was my nana's.'

I winced. *Shut up, Izzy. Shut up!* He doesn't want to know about your old nan's handbag.

He smiled. 'It's very beautiful.'

'Yes,' I said, suddenly feeling grateful that it was dark. It was uncomfortable looking at him so directly so I turned away slightly and pretended to survey the view.

'Amazing, isn't it?' he said, but he didn't avert his eyes from my face and I felt them on me, watching me closely.

'Yes,' I said again, wondering if I might say something with more than one syllable in it.

'You could never get bored of that view, could you?'

'No,' I said, putting an end to that wonder.

I had to get a grip. Now was not the time to mumble my way through a disjointed conversation. I had to charm him with my scintillating, witty repartee. *Don't blow it, Izzy.*

'I'm lucky, I get to see it every day,' he continued, moving closer towards me. I felt awkward yet strangely excited by being near him. It wasn't a feeling I had ever felt before and, uncomfortable as it was, I didn't want it to stop. But in true Izzy style I wasn't sure what to say next so I said nothing and he said nothing and we just stood there both taking in the view for a moment.

'You managed to find the toilet then?' He smiled, his piercing eyes probing my face.

'Ye— um, yer. Thanks . . . I mean, yes, thanks. I did.' Oh my God. I had forgotten how to speak.

'I didn't mean to embarrass you with the whole "toilet girl" comment,' he said. 'It was a bit juvenile of me I know, but I was trying to get your attention.'

My attention? Why would he want to do that? He was far too important and cool-looking. Perhaps I had loo roll stuck to my shoe and he had wanted to warn me. I quickly looked down at my feet just in case but there was nothing there and I felt relieved.

From the fleeting glances I allowed myself, I could see his hair looked honey-coloured and longish, hanging loosely around his shoulders. He was wearing a white shirt that was slightly open and three-quarter length trousers that had huge patchwork pockets on them. I also noticed he had really cool beads round his neck. He was tall – but then next to me most people were – and he looked really tanned, as if he'd been on holiday for a while. I would've bet my allowance that he had a girlfriend, because he was just about the most gorgeous man I had ever seen.

'This your first time in Ibiza?' he asked, still smiling warmly.

'Can you tell?' I replied, thinking that I might just graduate to multi-syllables or – shock horror – even full sentences anytime now.

'Hmm,' he said, laughing, and I laughed a little too.

'Enjoying the party?'

'It's OK, yeah.'

He looked at me quizzically, as if he was waiting for me to say something else.

'Just OK?'

'No, better than OK. Great. Really cool.' I tried to sound more enthusiastic because I sensed that he wanted me to.

'You like the music?'

'Yeah. I mean, it's cool . . . I suppose I'm more of an indie girl really though . . .' As soon as the words left my lips I instantly regretted them. Hadn't he been standing behind the DJ booth when he had shouted to me over the mike? This meant in all probability he was either really good friends with the DJ or the DJ himself. *Oh nooooo.*

'An indie girl, eh? I play guitar a bit. What bands are you into?'

I felt silly talking about it but said: 'I quite like The Dude Sound . . .' Which, considering I owned every CD they'd ever released, was an honorary member of their online fan club and had been to see them four times in the last twelve months, was a bit of an understatement.

'*I'm nothing without the smile on her face, my life without the kiss of her lips, empty and out of place . . .*'

Oh my God, he was quoting 'Without Her', my favourite ever Dude Sound track.

Who *was* this guy?

'I'm a big fan,' he said.

'They're my favourite band!' I said, and then worried that it had sounded really childish. 'I've been to see them a few times back home.'

'Where's home then?' he asked.

'In England,' I said, laughing. 'No listen, I'm just being facetious. I'm from London.' I was chuffed I'd managed to include an adult word like 'facetious' into the conversation. I thought it made me sound intelligent and funny, and thankfully he laughed.

I wanted to ask him where he was from too, because I detected a sort of soft, northern-ish accent, but I couldn't be sure and didn't have the courage to ask.

'You been here long?'

Did he mean at the party or in Ibiza?

'Umm, I'm in Ibiza for three weeks,' I said, hoping I picked the right answer to the right question. I didn't *really* want him to think I was facetious. 'It's only my second day here today.'

'Wow! You must be pretty special, getting an invite to one of Alfredo's infamous parties.'

'Well, my – my *friend*, she knows him. She's been to a few of these parties before . . .' I said, putting on my best 'I'm always at these kinds of parties having these types of conversations with devastatingly fit men' voice.

Something had stopped me from telling him about my sister though. I knew that if I mentioned her he'd probably want to meet her, and when he did he'd instantly fall in love with her like everyone else did and wouldn't look at me again. Right now, the thought of that was too much to bear, so I kind of lied. Also, he'd know that if she was my sister, I must be younger than her, and I didn't fancy letting on that I was only sixteen (almost seventeen). He looked a bit older and I didn't want to put him off me in case he did actually like me a bit – even if that was a remote possibility.

'So, what are your plans for the holiday then?' he asked, sounding genuinely interested.

I desperately tried to think of something to say that might make me sound exotic and intriguing so he would want to carry on talking to me.

'Well, I – aside from the sunbathing, cocktails and clubbing, I'm going to check out the beach tomorrow,' I said, making it up as I went along.

He looked at me, his head cocked to one side.

'Ah, a beach babe, huh? The beaches here are amazing: Las Salinas, Cala Carbo . . . Playa d'en Bossa . . . My favourite is Cala Jondal, though. I go for a run there every day, blow a few cobwebs away, keep fit, you know . . . Who are you going to the beach with?'

'I don't know yet,' I said, lowering my eyes and finding myself uncharacteristically flirting. I wasn't surprised that he went running every day. He was *so* fit and I could tell, even through his shirt, that he had an amazing body.

'I do,' he said, a smile creeping across his face.

'Who?' I asked, shyly.

'Me,' he said, matter-of-fact. 'You're going to the beach with me.'

I met his gaze for a second.

'Am I?'

'Yes,' he replied. 'You are.'

'And do I have a choice in that?' I asked, clearly flirting now.

'No,' he said softly. 'None whatsoever.'

I felt my stomach flip over and my knees go a bit weak. All this flirty banter, it was *so* not me.

'Do you dive?' he suddenly asked, breaking the moment.

'Dive? Well, er, no not really,' I said, not wanting to let on that I was a bit scared of heights and that I always held my nose whenever I jumped into a swimming pool.

'I can teach you if you like.'

I suddenly had visions of myself spectacularly belly-flopping in front of him, making a total prat of myself.

'I'm a little scared of heights – and water,' I confessed.

'I promise not to let you drown,' he said, smiling.

But I wouldn't have minded if it meant *him* rescuing me.

'If you fancy it, we could head down to Cala Jondal beach tomorrow,' he said.

In my mind I was screaming *Yes! Yes! I'd love to! Let's go right now!* but instead I said, 'OK, why not? Although I have to tell you, my running is about as great as my diving.'

He laughed. 'No running, we'll just chill out. I could pick you up on my moped maybe.'

Moped! This conversation was getting better by the second. I'd always fancied a boyfriend with his own transport, even though I knew I was getting way ahead of myself even thinking about him being my boyfriend.

'Listen, give me your number and I'll call you,' he said.

My heart sank a little. I'd been here before with the 'I'll call you' line. Lads would take my number and then I'd wait for a call that never came. Was it something I'd said? Something I *hadn't* said? Did they say they'd call because they didn't want to hurt my feelings, even when they had no intention of actually ever calling?

'Give me yours and then take mine just in case,' he suggested, as if sensing that I didn't believe him. 'I'm DJing at another party at Café Del Sol tomorrow night. It's more of a chilled thing than tonight – maybe you'd like to come after we've been to the beach, you can bring your mates too . . .' His green eyes were shining and I found myself wondering what it would be like to look right into them up close. I opened my broken bag and reached for my phone, which was covered in silly glitter stickers and photos and pink stick-on gemstones, and suddenly seemed really babyish. I went to 'add contacts' and realised I didn't even know his name.

'It's Rex,' he said, 'Rex Brown,' which scared me as I really was beginning to think he could read my mind now. I tried to punch in his number, which was proving difficult as it felt like someone had removed the bones from my fingers, making them all floppy like Pot Noodle, but I made sure I saved it before giving him mine.

'Well, it's been a pleasure to meet you,' he said, suddenly reaching up towards my face with his hand and very gently brushing a strand of hair from my eyes. Even though I was sure this was just a friendly gesture, I was taken aback nonetheless and began tingling all over. 'I'm really glad I did.' And I noticed he was giving me a funny look which wasn't that dissimilar to the look Toby Parker had given me that time I'd told him to follow his heart and his dreams of being a professional footballer. I couldn't help but take it to be a bad sign. 'I've got to get back as my next set is up and —'

'Of course,' I said, inwardly cringing about the whole 'I'm such an indie girl' cock-up I'd made earlier. I reckon I had more chance of winning the next British Diving Championships than I had of him calling me.

'I'll leave you with the view then,' he said, smiling as he turned and began to walk away.

'It was nice to meet you too,' I called out. I watched him walk off for a few seconds and was mortified when he turned round and caught me still looking.

'Hope to see you soon, Isabelle!' he called back to me, waving in the distance.

When he was firmly out of sight I wrapped my arms

around my chest and hugged myself, unable to stifle the huge grin on my face. I'd just met an amazing, gorgeous boy – well, man actually – and he was a DJ and owned a moped and was going to call me and take me to the beach. Or so he said. But even if he didn't, it was nice that he'd said it in the first place, which was almost enough for me.

I looked out at the view before me again and somehow it seemed even more beautiful than before. The lights seemed to shine even brighter beneath me. I breathed in the air deeply in an attempt to help me to stop shaking and keep calm. It was getting chillier now, but inside I felt a soft, warm glow, quickly followed by panic.

'Where the hell have you been?' Ellie barked, giving me her worried face as she came marching towards me. 'I've been everywhere searching for you! I mean it, Izzy, don't do that. I've spent half the bloody night asking people if they've seen you. I told you not to slope off on your own.'

I said I was sorry and that I just got lost on my way back from the toilet, which was sort of true. I didn't want to tell her about my meeting with Rex. She'd only tell the others and they'd all tease me about it. Besides, he had seemed a bit older than me and he had a moped, and I was worried that Ellie would disapprove of both those things.

I contemplated texting Willow to tell her what had happened, but was too busy replaying the whole conversation I'd just had with Rex in my head, like you do a favourite scene in a film: what he'd said, what I'd said, his facial expressions, the way he'd gone to brush the hair from my face and how it had made me tingle ... 'It's been a pleasure to meet you . . . Hope to see you soon, Isabelle!'

And it took me a whole five minutes or so of playing it all back in my mind over and over and over again to realise that, actually, I hadn't even told him my name.

Chapter 4

Sunlight streamed in through the window the next morning, giving the bedroom a soft glow and making me feel instantly alive and happy. I rubbed my eyes and looked at my phone, which I'd placed on the little table next to my bed so that it was close and I would hear it immediately if it beeped. *If* it beeped. There were no messages.

It's early, I thought to myself. *Don't stress, Izzy, don't stress.* But I knew the only thing on my mind that day would be him and the fact that he'd said he'd call.

It was pointless staying in bed. I was too full of nervous excitement, so I got up and padded quietly over to the doors that led to the balcony, so as not to wake Ellie, who was asleep in the bed next to me. I squinted as I stepped out on to the cool tiled floor. The sunlight was bright and the sky already blue and cloudless. I leaned over the balcony and took in a lungful of air as I yawned.

Although the apartment actually belonged to a friend of Narinda's family, she had not, as you might have thought, pulled rank and nabbed the best bedroom for herself. Instead we had tossed a coin to see who was going to sleep where and it transpired that I would be sharing with Ellie. I couldn't help but think that Ellie felt like she'd drawn the short straw. She had come on holiday to be with her friends, gossip about men and life and people they knew and stuff – not share a room with her little sister with whom, genetics aside, she had little in common with these days.

I wasn't entirely sure why Ellie had invited me to Ibiza in the first place. I knew it was on the pretext of it being my birthday soon and that this was sort of like her present to me, but I felt sure Mum had played a big part in goading her into bringing me.

I had always thought Ellie was the coolest since I was little. She taught me how to French skip, ride a bicycle and to apply mascara for the first time. My mum delights in reminding me of this one time when I was seven years old – I cried for three days solid because Ellie had gone to stay with a family friend for a long weekend. According to Jackson family legend, for that's what this story had now become, I had insisted on wearing a T-shirt that belonged to Ellie in protest at being kept from her – even sleeping in it and refusing to take it off until she had safely returned. I doted on her.

Then when Dad died it was as if I'd lost a sister as well. Ellie was seventeen at the time and had found a new state of independence, namely in the form of a clapped-out old Citroën 2CV car that Mum and Dad had bought for her on her seventeenth birthday. When she wasn't zipping off with her friends, she was hidden behind her bedroom door, studying or spending hours putting on make-up with her mates just to go to the cinema.

It wasn't that she was ever horrible to me; it was just

that as her life progressed into adulthood and – as I was now beginning to experience – the complications that this brought with it, she sort of forgot I was there, and I could only watch her breeze in and out of our house, always doing something and going somewhere fabulous, none of which involved me.

Rejected, I found myself coming up with elaborate ways to get her attention; I'd paint her pictures and make her collages out of pop-star photos that I found in magazines to try and impress her (hey, I was only eleven at the time, OK?) and if that didn't work I'd steal something from her bedroom so that she would *have* to talk to me, because being shouted at was preferable to being ignored. Sometimes I would sneak into her bedroom when she wasn't around and snoop about. Back then, Ellie's room was a place of forbidden pleasure and delight for me. The make-up and bottles of perfume that cluttered the small dressing table with the mirror; the pop-star posters adorning every inch of wall space; and, best of all, her underwear drawer filled with bras and expensive-looking lingerie (that probably weren't that expensive at all looking back). Ellie's room hinted at what life would one day be like for me, and this filled me with apprehension and excitement. The conversations I would have, the boys I would kiss, how I would sympathise with my girlfriends when they'd been cruelly dumped (clearly a predicament that would never happen to me) and how I would cheer them up by giving them a makeover.

Naturally, none of what I was feeling went unnoticed

by our beady-eyed, annoyingly astute mum. 'As you get older,' Mum had said, putting a comforting arm round my shoulders, 'you will catch up with her. And one day, when you're much older, you'll be best friends again,' she had reassured me, softly.

Now, on my first holiday alone with my sister – in Ibiza no less – I wanted to feel as though I'd finally arrived at that catch-up point. I knew this was my opportunity to show Ellie how much I had changed and who I had become. I wanted her to see that I could be clever and witty too, 'one of the girls', a bona fide member of the 'Ellie Jackson Hip Girl Squad' who had earned her rightful stripes. Only I didn't feel like that at all. I was simply Ellie's little sister, Izzy, and nothing had changed.

I relaxed on to one of the sun loungers on the balcony and found myself inadvertently smiling. The previous night's events were still running through my head and I wondered if it was too early to call Willow. I was desperate to tell her all about last night: the villa, the people, the music and – and Rex. *Oh God, Rex.* Just thinking about him made my skin tingle all over.

I had felt different since our meeting, lighter and more positive somehow. It was as if I was suddenly full of energy and vitality, high on life. Perhaps this was how you felt when you fell in love – but you can't fall in love after just five minutes of conversation with someone, can you?

I pulled my phone out of my robe pocket – it was coming everywhere with me today – and pressed Willow's number. I knew it was early to call, but being the gossip freak that she is, I figured she'd be so blown away by all my news that she'd soon forget it was only eight a.m.

'Wils?'

'Euuurggh . . .' there was a groaning sound as she picked up the phone.

'Wils, it's me – Izzy.' I found myself whispering so as not to wake Ellie.

'Iz – is that you?' Her voiced sounded croaky, like voices tend to do first thing in the morning. 'Oh my God, Iz, babes!' I heard a muffled noise like she was scrabbling around for something. 'Jeez, Iz! It's seven in the morning!'

'Wils, look, I'm sorry, shall I call you back? I totally forgot about the time difference and everything.'

'I'm awake now, you cow!' she said, and I imagined her sitting up in bed, not a hair out of place as usual. 'So, come on then, how's the party capital of the earth? Been clubbing yet? Is it, like, full of dead-fit boys? Tell all, I'm *dying* here!' She made a fake choking sound as if she was being strangled.

'We went to a private pool party at a huge villa last night,' I blathered excitedly, realising in my awestruck state that I had forgotten to take some pictures on my phone and send them to her. 'It was just the coolest thing *ever*. Everyone there looked so amazing and the music was brilliant – some of the best DJs in Ibiza were playing. And there was this huge great swimming pool in the middle of it all, and later on in the night people stripped down to their underwear and bikinis – can you believe it? – and just dived in. It was crazy, and we didn't come home until three a.m. and —'

'Slow down!' Willow shrieked. 'I'm lost already!'

It felt weird talking to Willow like this because, as a general rule, it was her who always had the amazing stories to tell. It was like our roles had been reversed, and I sensed that she felt odd about this too.

'So what are your plans today then?' she sighed. 'Slink around the pool, get a tan, and watch lots of fit lads playing volleyball on the beach?'

'Got to fit in with Ellie and that, I suppose. But I definitely hope to make it to the beach.'

Oh God. The beach. Would he really phone me?

'Must be bloody brilliant not having any parents around,' she mused.

There was a slight pause and then she said quietly: 'Joe and I are back on.'

This was not good news and I felt my heart sink. Since Wils had discovered about this girl Joe had been texting behind her back and dumped him, she had sworn she would rather sit *my* exams as well as her own before she would ever get back with him. But Joe knew which buttons to press to get back in her good books. He'd give her his sad eyes and promise he would treat her better and gradually he'd chip away at her until she would cave in. Willow was really just a big softy at heart.

'That's cool,' I said, although I knew she could probably tell I didn't really mean it. I couldn't help but wonder if she'd have ever got back with him if I'd have still been at home. Perhaps I could've talked her out of it, counteracted his 'I'll never mess you around again' speech by reminding her of all the times he'd let her down and put her second. I felt as though by not being there, to support her in her moments of weakness, I had let her down.

'Maybe it'll be different this time round,' I said optimistically, wanting to be happy for her.

'Yeah, maybe,' she said, unconvincingly. 'Anyway, you've got to keep me updated on the holiday. I want to know *everything* that happens, especially boy-wise,' she demanded.

'That reminds me,' I said, sensing now was the right time to tell her about *him*.

But all of a sudden my phone made this strange bleeping noise.

'Wils —' *beep, beep, beep* 'I think I'm in lo—' I said, as the line went dead.

Chapter 5

Ellie was stretched out on a sun lounger, looking typically gorgeous, as Louisa rubbed sun lotion on to her back.

'We're staying here for a while and then maybe heading off to the beach,' Ellie said, pushing her sunglasses back off of her face and squinting up at me. 'Fancy coming?'

The midday sun was beating down hard and the tiles felt hot under my feet.

'I need to find a shop that sells phone credit,' I replied, ignoring her earlier question – not out of rudeness, but because I wanted to keep my options open in case Rex had other plans. 'Can I get you guys anything while I'm there?'

'I think the shop down the road sells phone credit,' piped up Charlotte, who was carefully rubbing oil on to her long legs and adjusting her colourful headscarf.

'Thanks,' I said as I pulled on an old T-shirt and quickly wrapped a sarong around my waist. I *had* to get to the shops. What if he texted me or left a message and I couldn't retrieve it because I had no credit? This was a total disaster. He might think I was blanking him.

I skipped down the steps and on to the main street towards the local parade of shops.

San Antonio, where we were staying, was buzzing with people on their way to or from the beach; groups of girls looking tanned and sexy in their minuscule bikinis and shorts hung outside the cafés that littered the main drag, and guys on mopeds sped past beeping at them and waving.

I didn't want to go too far as I was worried I might not be able to find my way back to the apartment, so I walked up a bit towards the shop that was selling crazy lilos in the shape of crocodiles and bananas.

'Phone credit, *por favor* . . .' I said, pleased with myself that I'd managed to say something in Spanish other than '*gracias*'. The man behind the counter stared at me blankly.

'Er . . . phone?' I said, holding up my mobile in the hope that he'd understand what I was trying to say.

More blank looks.

'I look round,' I said, suddenly wishing I'd taken up Spanish as a subject at school. My eyes darted round the shop, past the chocolate bars with foreign-sounding names, brightly-coloured beach towels and cheap sunglasses, but there was nothing that suggested they sold phone credit. It was no good, I'd have to run back and get Ellie.

'Looking for something?' an oddly familiar voice suddenly said from behind me, making me jump.

It was him. Oh *noooo*. He was standing in front of me, a bike helmet under one arm and a tall blonde girl linked in his other. He looked even more gorgeous than I had remembered, if that was possible.

'Hi!' I said shakily, in a state of total panic and shock – not the best combination when you're trying to look cool. Was this man destined to sneak up on me all my life?

'Need a hand?' he asked, smiling.

'No, thanks. I'm just erm, looking for some, er, milk. Run out of milk,' I stammered lamely. There was no way I was letting on about the phone credit. He might think I was desperate to make sure I didn't miss his call, if indeed he was planning to call. Besides, I was more interested in the girl holding his arm. She had to be his girlfriend. She was tall and gorgeous with long slim legs that went on for ever and she had that effortless chic look about her. I felt sick. Why couldn't I have been wearing something half decent, like the cute denim mini I'd brought, or at least something that matched my sarong instead of this baggy old T-shirt that had a smiley face on it ironically saying, *Don't worry, be happy*.

'You must think I'm stalking you,' he said, meeting my gaze for a second.

If only.

'This is Jo-Jo,' Rex said, gesturing towards the beautiful girl next to him.

'Hi!' I said as brightly as I could.

She looked me up and down in an unfriendly manner and linked her arm into his more tightly.

'We've not long been back from the party. I'm going off to the gym for a bit of a workout and then heading to the beach later to chill out,' he said, and I was suddenly besieged with the vision of him looking all gorgeous and working up a sweat on the treadmill. It made me even more flustered.

'Cool.' *Oh no, here come the monosyllabic answers again,* I thought, so I added, 'I had a really great time last night.'

'Me too,' he said.

We stared at each other for a second and Jo-Jo suddenly

said, 'Rex, I'm just going to get some water. You want some?'

'I'm good,' he replied, and I was relieved when she dropped his arm and walked off towards the cooler.

'I guess it saved me a phone call,' he said, 'now that we've bumped into each other.'

'Oh yeah, right, I guess so.'

This was just awful. I wished I could start the whole morning again. It had been so perfect just thinking about him, holding on to the memory of last night. I was so excited about the possibility of seeing him again. I had premonitions of me looking fantastic and gorgeous, the pair of us hanging out together at the beach, the gentle wind in our hair and sun on our skin as we messed around in the sea . . . but instead here I was sandwiched between these funny half-naked statues with *Ibiza Forever* written on them and banana inflatables, in my oldest, baggiest T-shirt, and him linking arms with a model-type girl looking like something out of a shampoo advert. Could it have been any worse?

I could tell he sensed I was uncomfortable.

'Jo-Jo's a mate . . .' he said, and I seriously wondered if in fact my thoughts were being projected above my head in a giant speech bubble for all to see.

'I gave her a lift back from the party to San Antonio, where she's staying.'

I sensed he was trying to make a point that he and Jo-Jo weren't an item and I felt that strange rush of excitement.

'So, do you fancy the beach later?' he said, his beautiful green eyes shining. 'I promise you don't have to do any diving if you don't want to.'

'I'd really love to,' I said, wondering if I sounded too keen. 'Maybe I'll just watch you dive from a distance.'

'You can give me marks out of ten,' he smiled broadly and I sensed relief in his voice, which gave me hope about the whole Jo-Jo and bad T-shirt thing.

'Whereabouts are you staying? I'll pick you up.'

'I'm . . . we're up at —' and then I suddenly thought about Ellie and Co. and the last thing I wanted was for them to find out I was meeting a guy and heading off to the beach with him. They'd only ask questions and want to meet him, and it would be embarrassing with Ellie doing the whole 'look after her' big-sister act. So I said, 'I'll meet you outside here if it's easier.'

'OK,' he said. 'I'll pick you up here at three. And you don't mind the bike?' he asked, gesturing to his moped outside. Mind? I was ecstatic! I'd never been on a moped before, let alone one that belonged to a drop-dead gorgeous DJ.

'No, that's cool,' I said casually. I was getting good at doing casual.

'Three it is then.'

'Bye.'

I waited a few seconds for him to leave before I raced out of the shop.

'You want phone card?' the man said to me as I was leaving, but I ignored him.

It was nearly midday. I had three hours to decide what I was going to wear. And what excuse was I going to make to Ellie about sloping off all afternoon? *You'll think of something, Izzy,* I told myself as I broke into a run.

Chapter 6

I knew I should probably just tell the truth: tell Ellie that I'd met this guy and that he wanted to take me to the beach. I knew Ellie would freak if she found out I was going to ride on his moped, and she'd probably doubly freak if she knew he was a bit older than me, even though I wasn't sure exactly by how much. I didn't like the idea of lying to Ellie, but I justified it as a necessity so as not to cause her any worry. Anyway, I had to actually *think* of a lie first.

I decided to go for a bit of a dip to cool down and get my thoughts together. I got back, dumped *the* T-shirt and walked over towards the pool, adjusting my new yellow crochet bikini that Mum had bought me. *Perhaps I'll wear it to meet Rex*, I thought as I eased myself into the water and started to swim. Yeah, my crochet yellow bikini and my denim mini. Hopefully he'd look at me and think I was a real babe, even though I wasn't exactly chuffed at the thought of him seeing my wobbly bits.

I dipped my head underwater and let the coolness surround me. I loved swimming, even if I wasn't very good at it and was a bit nervous in deep water. One of my dreams was to swim with dolphins, and I imagined myself holding on to their fins as they glided gracefully through the water and I how I would be free from worries such as which bikini to wear or what lies to tell.

What was I going to say to Ellie?

I wished I had got that phone credit now, as I knew that if I called Willow she'd come up with something at the drop of a hat and —

'Oops! Sorry!'

I'd bumped into someone as I came up for air and had knocked them off their crocodile-shaped lilo.

I gave them a hand back up on to it.

'No worries,' said the girl, flashing me a friendly smile. I figured she was a bit younger than me, although I couldn't be sure because her hair was all over her face.

'I was in a world of my own.'

'You can borrow it if you like,' she said, smiling at me in an over-zealous manner.

'Eh?'

'The lilo.'

'Oh no, it's fine. Cool lilo though,' I said, just for something to say, because I didn't really think it was that cool at all.

'Yeah, my dad got it for me. Embarrassing, isn't it?'

'Well, that's what dads are for.' I laughed and wondered how I knew that, because I didn't really have much experience when it came to embarrassing fathers. I'd not quite reached that awkward stage of being totally ashamed by my parents' presence when my dad had died. He was still just my big, cuddly old dad, someone I looked up to and who held me in his arms when I was scared.

I suddenly felt jealous of this girl's ability to be ashamed of her dad. I would've given anything to have the chance to feel that way about my dad. My stomach wrenched with the realisation that I would never hide my head in shame or cringe with humiliation like other girls my age did when their dads would come to collect them from parties, or showed them any affection in front of their mates, or bought them stupid lilos. All these feelings, and more, I would forever be denied.

'I'm Edie, by the way,' said the girl in front of me, snapping me out of my thoughts.

'I'm Izzy,' I smiled at her. 'Good to meet you.'

'You too. You here with your folks?' she asked.

'Well, my sister and her friends,' I replied, looking over in the direction of Ellie and Co.

'Lucky you,' she rolled her eyes. 'My parents have been driving me bonkers.'

She looked like she was struggling with the lilo now, so I reached out to help her keep it steady. 'Fancy grabbing a Coke?' she said. I looked around briefly to see if I could catch Ellie's attention, but she was still horizontal so I thought, *Why not?* It's not like I needed her permission. So I carried on with Edie towards the bar and she promptly ordered two Cokes and told the barman to put them on her dad's tab.

'Thanks,' I said, taking a gulp and getting a proper look at her. Edie was a bit shorter and stockier than me, if that was humanly possible. Her shoulder-length brown hair was straight, although it was difficult to tell as it was wet and hanging round her shoulders in straggles. Her face was all smiley and round, and there was a smattering of freckles across her nose that made it look as though someone had sprinkled her with brown sugar. I noticed she was wearing a T-shirt over her bikini and I wondered if it was for the same reasons I wore T-shirts over mine – because she was self-conscious.

'Ibiza's great, isn't it?' she said, wiping the strands of hair from her face. 'Have you been clubbing yet? There's no way Mum and Dad would let me go on my own and there's no way they're coming with me thanks very much, I'd die of shame. How old are you?' She didn't even draw breath.

'I'm seventeen,' I managed to say. Well, I was *almost* seventeen and lying about a couple of months wasn't going to hurt was it? Besides, I needed the practice.

'Wow. I'm fourteen, fifteen in three months. Are you still at school? Where are you from? I wish I could go to some of the clubs out here, they look *amaaaazing*, but instead I have to go to dinner with my parents every night and watch them drink themselves delirious on sangria and get all giggly and act stupid. Thank God I bought my headphones with me or else I'd corpse with boredom.'

I wasn't sure which question to answer first.

'I'm from London and I'm just about to start Sixth Form College and I have been clubbing already – well, sort of – and I'm off to the beach this afternoon.' *With him.*

'Am I jealous or what,' Edie said with a smile and I thought how pretty her face was, even if it was a bit on the chubby side.

'Perhaps we can hang out together?' she asked, hopefully. 'You'd be saving me from the holiday from hell.'

'Yeah,' I replied, weakly, feeling a bit sorry for her. 'That would be great.'

'Nice one!' she squealed. 'Why don't you come and meet my parents. They'll be cool letting me go off with you if they meet you and realise you're, like, a bit older and everything.'

'Er, well, I'm not sure . . .'

This was the last thing I needed. I'd come away for the first time on my own and now I was going to be lumbered with someone else's parents.

'That way, I won't have to watch my dad making a total prat of himself on the pedaloes down at Cala Jondal this afternoon.'

Cala Jondal? Wasn't that the beach *he* wanted to show me? A bad thought crept into my head. What if I *did* go over and meet her parents? Then I could introduce them to Ellie and tell her I was going to the beach with them, and then think up some last-minute excuse not to go, but still tell Ellie I was going with them anyway. It was perfect! Oh, but hang on, what if Edie saw me down at Cala Jondal? Then she'd know I had lied and I'd feel terrible because she looked so happy that I'd agreed to hang out with her. I guess I could always say I'd changed my mind and had come to look for her. Besides, I figured Cala Jondal was probably quite a big beach and it was unlikely I'd bump into her.

'I'd love to meet your parents,' I said, already feeling guilty that I was just using her as an excuse. *I'll make it up to her*, I told myself. *I'll hang out with her tomorrow.*

Chapter 7

I almost ran down to the lilo shop, crossing my fingers that Ellie and Co. wouldn't come back from the beach too early, or worse, run into Edie and her family on their way to Cala Jondal, which undoubtedly would have been very awkward indeed. But I was there already and my heart was racing so fast again that I thought I might suddenly keel over.

Edie had introduced me to her mum and dad and her little brother, Sammy, and in turn I'd introduced them to Ellie, who thought it was great that I'd made a friend and she seemed happy for me to go to the beach with them. 'It's cool, babes, do whatever you want,' she'd said, although I sensed a slight disappointment in her voice. 'We're planning to be at the beach for a while, maybe even go on one of those banana boat thingummywotsits. You know those long yellow inflatable boats that take you out to sea that spin you round until you fall off?'

I could tell she was trying to tempt me to go with them.

'I've agreed to hang out with Edie now,' I said, suddenly feeling a little reticent.

'Well, suit yourself,' Ellie said, more cheerily this time. 'Have fun then.'

They seemed so nice, Edie's family, and I'd felt a grade-A bitch having to run down to her apartment a few minutes before leaving to meet *him* to tell her I couldn't make it after all.

She'd looked so dejected that I almost couldn't go through with it, and I promised her I would hang out with her tomorrow, and in the meantime would she like to borrow my Dude Sound CD, which was a good move as she smiled a bit when I'd said that, even though I could tell she didn't believe me when I said I was sick and was going to rest up in the apartment.

After ten minutes of waiting I was beginning to think this was all some big joke at my expense and that my fears of him just saying he wanted to meet me and not really meaning it were true. Who had I been kidding? What would a guy as gorgeous and cool as him see in me anyway when there were girls like Jo-Jo on the planet? I was just about to turn round and go straight back to the apartment when he pulled up right in front of me, causing me to take two steps sharply back. He tugged the helmet off his head, letting his gorgeous glossy hair tumble down in waves around his shoulders.

'Your carriage awaits, my lady,' he said with a smile, and did this sort of half-bow thing, which made me giggle nervously. 'You ready to ride?'

'Sure am!' And I found myself hopping on to the back of his bike excitedly and putting on the spare helmet he had given me.

'Hold on!' he said, and I wrapped my arms tightly around his waist, and he felt warm and firm and I could feel his chest move up and down beneath his white T-shirt as he breathed. Being that close to him gave me a strange tingling feeling in my stomach like a thousand butterflies trying to escape. And it felt good. Weird maybe, but definitely good.

Being on the back of his bike was just the most

exhilarating feeling ever. I was terrified and gripped him with a force, especially when we went round any corners, which made me feel like I might come flying off like a frisbee. I watched, mesmerised, as Ibiza shot past me in a blur of vivid colours, the azure-blue of the sky and the smoky-brown dustiness of the road melding with flashes of green and orange from the trees bearing their brightly-coloured fruit. We were heading along a straight road that was lined with small whitewashed houses and open stretches of land littered with olive groves. Now I knew why people raved about being on the back of a bike so much – it was such a buzz.

I knew it was wrong to go on the back of his moped and not tell anyone, but somehow, despite the fact that I had lied to my sister, it seemed so right. Like it was meant to be.

Perhaps if I had just explained to Ellie how important this date with Rex was to me she would've given me her blessing, even been happy for me, but it was a risk I was too scared to take. Besides, Mum had made her put her hand on her heart and promise to look after me, 'Girl Guides' Honour,' and I was pretty sure that this didn't include allowing me to ride on the back of an older guy's moped and go off to the beach with him alone, even if there would be loads of people there and I instinctively trusted him.

We carried on up towards some mountains and I wondered if we were anywhere near Alfredo's villa, where we'd been the night before.

'Not far now,' I thought I heard him say, although I was in no hurry for the journey to end, as I figured this might be the only time I could legitimately hold on to him so tightly.

We finally stopped at the edge of a small road and to the right of me I saw the stretch of white sand dotted with pine trees and the clear sea twinkling in the sunshine.

'Wow, it looks so beautiful,' I said, taking in the view.

'The view from where I'm standing is pretty good too,' he said, turning to look at me. No one had ever really told me I was beautiful before and his remark filled me with confidence. If someone as gorgeous and cool as Rex thought *I* could possibly be beautiful, then maybe I really was.

He opened the compartment at the back of the bike and pulled out a small picnic basket and a blanket. 'Provisions!' he said, smiling at me. We held each other's gaze nervously, but I didn't look away first; I was scared it might break the magic.

'Come on, race you!' he said, sprinting off.

We ran down towards the beach like a couple of little kids and I thought I might collapse with happiness – or heat exhaustion – before we got to the bottom.

'This is my favourite beach ever,' he said catching his breath as we finally made it to the sand. 'I learned to dive here and, when I can, I come running here every morning, just as the sun comes up.'

'Wow, that's dedicated,' I said. The last time I ran for anything was the number 32 bus that took me to school. 'I can see why it would be your favourite,' I said, taking in the idyllic surroundings. Cala Jondal was a beautiful white stretch of beach surrounded by more pebbly parts. It was quiet and relaxed with just a few sun worshippers scattered around taking shade under the pine trees, and small groups of people chilling out playing volleyball and swimming in the sea.

'Let's go up to my favourite place,' he said and I slipped my gold flip-flops off and held them in my hand as I followed, watching him. He was wearing some cut-off denim shorts just below the knee; they looked old and soft with frayed edges and had a patch on the back pocket that made them look even more careworn and cool. His white T-shirt covered his chest and set off his deeply-tanned arms well, and he was wearing blue-and-white striped pool shoes that I knew must be really trendy because I'd noticed other lads wearing them at Alfredo's party the night before. I saw he still had the beads on that he'd been wearing when we'd met and I made a mental note to myself to remember to ask him about them, as well as the whole how-he-knew-my-name-without-me-ever-telling-him business.

After a few minutes we approached what looked like a small cave, and Rex turned to me and took my hand – mainly I thought to help me over the small rocks that led the way into it.

'Take a seat,' he said, as he pulled off his T-shirt and laid down the blanket he'd been carrying. I turned away, embarrassed by the sight of him undressing.

'I brought refreshments! Lassi and water,' he said, pulling some bottles out of the basket to show me. I had no idea what lassi was, so I just smiled and said, 'Great.'

'And nectarines and grapes. I wasn't sure what you liked so I just grabbed some fruit from the market on the way here. Oh! And I bought some cheese and crackers too. Do you like cheese?' he asked. And then he stopped and shook his head and started to laugh. 'God, I'm such a smoothy, eh?

"Do you like cheese?" How's that for a chat-up line?'

I giggled. He was doing that thing I do where I cringe at the things I say, and it made me feel relaxed.

'It was a time for romance . . . Their eyes met across a crowded beach and he enticed her into his heart with promises of diamonds and – cheese and crackers,' he said, mocking himself, putting on a deep, dramatic voice like the ones you hear on trailers for films.

I creased up laughing.

'Don't be daft, I love cheese!' I said, even though I had to admit the conversation was taking a rather ridiculous turn.

He punched the air in victory. 'It's a winner! The lady loves cheese! She is powerless to resist his charms – and cheddar!'

We were both really laughing now and I tried not to stare at his bare, tanned chest as he produced all this wonderful stuff from the basket.

I realised I would have to do the same – strip off, I mean. I couldn't just lie there in the sweltering heat dressed in a top and denim skirt. But when I attempted to unbutton my skirt, I found I had completely lost the strength in my wrists and my hands kept slipping.

'I'm just going to test the water,' he said, his eyes scanning me softly. 'It's bound to be perfect swimming temperature . . .'

He walked off in the direction of the sea and left me standing there, inside this little shady alcove with a basket of goodies that he'd so thoughtfully brought along. I thought perhaps I'd been involved in a plane crash on the way to Ibiza and that really I'd died and that this was my life as I had always imagined it to be. He had sensed I was nervous about undressing and had made an excuse so I wouldn't have to suffer the mortal pain of doing it in front of him. I wondered if he was perhaps the most perfect man I had ever met. I took the advantage anyway, and when he was out of sight I frantically slipped my top over my head and wriggled out of my denim mini and hoped that if I closed my eyes and wished hard enough I might somehow miraculously gain a figure like Ellie's by the time he came back from the sea. Failing that, a sarong would've done, and I could've kicked myself for not remembering to bring one. But it was too late. As he returned, I realised I was standing there as good as in my underwear, and I suddenly felt very exposed.

'The sea is perfect,' he said, his skin glistening with tiny water droplets. I sat down on the soft blanket he'd brought along and attempted to adjust my body in the most flattering pose possible, even though no matter how I lay my thighs seemed to spread like margarine. I noticed him looking at me – not staring, just glancing – and I wondered if he was thinking, 'Wow, check out those thunder thighs.'

'You're embarrassed,' he said, smiling at me gently.

I was *so* embarrassed I wanted to dig a hole in the sand and hide in it.

'Don't be,' he said. 'You look fantastic in your bikini – a real beach goddess!'

Goddess? More like a big ice cream blob melting in the sun, but I felt thrilled that he had said it. The fact that he'd brought my body fear out into the open had made it seem less of an issue, and I found myself relaxing slightly.

'Perfection, dear lady, is in the eye of the beholder,' he said in a mock-plummy accent. I could feel he was looking at me intensely, so I looked at him too and our eyes scanned each other's faces. 'Do you know what I mean?' he asked, putting on a jokey cockney accent this time.

'Yes,' I replied, allowing myself to look into his green eyes properly, like I had wanted to do the night we met, but had been too shy. 'I know exactly what you mean. But then it's easy for you to say. You swim and dive and work out at the gym everyday.'

We both smiled and looked away, leaving the tension between us hanging in the air for a second.

'So, what do you think of the beach then?' he said after a few moments' silence, his normal accent resumed.

'It's the most beautiful beach I've seen,' I said, adding, 'although I haven't really been to many beaches in Ibiza.' And when I said 'many', what I really meant was 'any'.

'I come here to think as well as run,' he said, thoughtfully, 'when things get a bit hectic and I need time to reflect. Sometimes it's therapeutic to be alone with your thoughts and chill out, especially in a place as beautiful as this.'

He took a swig of his water and I wondered what he could want to reflect about, on the beach, alone. Past girlfriends maybe? Jo-Jo perhaps?

'Have you lived in Ibiza a long time?' I had held back asking him too many questions and by now I was desperate to know everything about him.

'About five years. I came here on holiday and never left. Fell in love with the place on sight,' he said, looking at me in a strange way and smiling. I couldn't tell whether he was teasing me or if he was actually suggesting – no, he couldn't be. It was ridiculous to think that he'd fallen in love with *me* at first sight.

'Really? What did your parents think about you staying?' I asked, wishing I hadn't, because it made me sound like I couldn't do anything without my parents' permission.

'Oh, you know, they were a bit freaked out at first but once they'd been out to see me, they were cool. They fell in love with the place too. But then, that's Ibiza. It's got magical properties and once you've been here you don't want to leave.'

I was beginning to understand what he meant.

'So how old were you when you first came here on holiday?' I asked, thinking that it was a pretty clever way of finding out his age.

'Young,' he said, smiling a little at the memory and continuing to hold my gaze, 'I was twenty-one.'

Now I'm not exactly great at maths, as my school report will testify, but even I could work out that this made him twenty-six years old. Oh. My. God. Twenty-six!

I didn't know why I was so surprised. I'd guessed he was a bit older than me, maybe twenty-three at most – but twenty-six! If he thought twenty-one was young, what would he make of me being sixteen? This was, as Willow would say, a twenty-four carat disaster (or in this case, twenty-six). So far he hadn't guessed I was that much younger, and I felt sure he would be put off if I told him my real age. Even if I hadn't been sure of his reaction, I wasn't prepared to find out, not since this was fast turning out to be the most special day of my sixteen (almost seventeen) years on this planet so far. Why spoil it now?

'I was pretty bored with life back in England,' he continued, rolling over on to his side and moving in a little closer to me, causing my heart to start pounding loudly in my chest again. I hoped he couldn't hear it, being that close to me and all. 'The rat-race,' he said, 'it's not really me.'

'And what is *you*?' I asked him, our bodies almost touching now. I was looking right into his eyes and noticed they were flecked with tiny bits of brown.

He broke my gaze and looked down for a moment. I wondered if I was asking him too many questions, but I felt so comfortable around him that I couldn't help myself.

He grabbed a handful of grapes and popped one into my mouth and then one in his own. It tasted delicious. 'Music is me,' he said thoughtfully, chewing on the grape. 'Music and friends and family and – being with people I love, I suppose.'

The mere mention of the word 'love' sent my head into a spin and I began to play with the beading on the ties of my bikini nervously.

We sat looking at each other for a second, neither of us saying anything. It wasn't uncomfortable exactly, but I sensed a tension, like he wanted to elaborate on what he'd just said, but wasn't sure whether to or not.

'Shall we go for a swim?' he finally said, breaking the moment. 'I don't know about you, but I'm feeling quite warm.'

'That's a great idea,' I said and he took my hand to pull me up.

So I discovered that Rex Brown was twenty-six and originally from Aldersley Hedge, a little village just outside Manchester – which kind of accounted for the soft lilt in his voice – and that he came to Ibiza five years ago with his friend, Steve, and a box of records and had never looked back. A few years of DJing in 'dives', as he had put it, paved the way to better clubs and bigger audiences and within a couple of years, the pair of them were playing to massive crowds and had earned themselves superstar DJ status.

He was a keen swimmer, diver and runner, and worked-out at the local gym. He liked fishing – everything to do with the sea in fact, and he dreamed of owning his own boat one day. Like me, he was an animal-lover and missed his family dog, Benjy, who he'd grown up with back home.

Even though I was reluctant to give away too much, we talked a bit about me too, and I told him all about my plans to become a vet, or at least work with animals somehow. I also mentioned my ambition to swim with dolphins and he said he wasn't surprised by that because I seemed like a very spiritual woman and dolphins are very spiritual creatures indeed. It felt great that he'd used the word 'woman', because it made me feel mature and slightly exotic and gave me the confidence to talk some more about myself. I was terrified he'd ask me how old I was and I kept waiting for him to bring it up but he didn't – which was kind of a relief, but also made me feel a bit bad too, because even though

I figured that not saying anything was not exactly the same thing as lying, in my heart I knew that it probably was.

We'd been walking and talking so much that until I had mentioned the dolphins, we had clean forgotten about that swim we were supposed to be having.

'Ladies first!' he said, gesturing towards the glittering crystal water as we finally approached the sea.

'Chicken!' I laughed as I waded out up to my knees. The water was warm and clear, like a bath, so I went out a little further and broke into a swim.

He followed, swimming towards me and suddenly he was right up close to me, holding me by the waist and gently moving me up through the water.

Just his touch sent ripples of excitement through me and I couldn't help giggling, which I hoped didn't sound too girly and stupid.

We swam around a bit and he splashed me, sending the salty water cascading over my head, and I screamed to get away because I was worried my mascara might run as I'd forgotten to wear the waterproof stuff, but by now I was having way too much fun to care, panda-eyes or not.

'I'm DJing at a beach party tonight at Café Del Sol in San Antonio. Do you know it?' he asked.

I said I'd heard of it, just to sound like I was well up on the scene, but really I had no idea where or what it was.

'It's one of the most famous bars in Ibiza,' he said. 'It's on the beach in San Antonio, you know, not far from where you're staying.' I nodded, thinking that this must be the beach that Ellie and gang had gone to today.

'The sunset there is so amazing, and if you haven't seen an Ibizan sunset before, well!' he said, mock-indignant. Before I could answer I suddenly lost my footing and momentarily slipped underwater. I began to cough violently as the salty water stung my throat.

'You OK?' he said, putting his hands on my shoulders and he looked so concerned that it was almost worth the embarrassment.

'I'm fine,' I spluttered, and realised I had lost my hairband and now my unruly mass of curls was hanging down in straggles around my face and shoulders. *How* attractive.

'You have the most amazing hair,' he said, staring at me.

I looked at him to see if he was being serious.

'What, this bird's nest?' I said, pointing to my head. 'You've got to be kidding.'

He stood still in the water and I realised that he could actually touch the bottom of the sea, unlike me.

'You're so not like all the other women I usually meet, do you know that?' he said, looking at me, his head cocked to one side.

'Why, do they all have straight hair then?' I smiled, knowing I was being facetious again, but kind of enjoying the fact that we were flirting again.

'*Touché*,' he said, laughing, but I wasn't sure if he was joking with me so I didn't answer.

'You're so, so . . . self-deprecating – it's very refreshing,' he said. 'But you shouldn't put yourself down, you've no need. You're lovely just as you are.'

Now I *really* didn't have a clue what he was on about. *Self-deprecating?*

As much as I wanted to accept that he was attempting to pay me a compliment, the fact that he'd mentioned 'other women' made me wonder whether he did this kind of thing all the time. Meet girls, whisk them off to the beach on his moped, feed them grapes and tell them they looked beautiful as he gave them the 'you're not like any of the other girls I meet' line. I mean, he was utterly stunning to look at *and* he was a DJ. Even *I* knew that this came with a bit of a reputation. He was bound to have girls flocking round him 24/7. Maybe he even had a girlfriend already? But something inside me sensed he wasn't a player. I couldn't be sure of course, but it was just a feeling I had when I looked into his eyes. They say that the eyes are the window to your soul, and when I looked into his, all I could see was honesty and kindness. Despite this, all these niggling doubts had got me thinking of Jo-Jo and I couldn't stop myself from asking about her.

'Did you manage to drop Jo-Jo off safely?' I asked, even though I already knew the answer.

'Yeah, she's going through a rough time at the moment. Her and Steve used to be an item until recently and – well, you know how these things go. Stuff happens. They split a week or so ago. She's pretty cut up, so I've been looking after her.'

He sounded quite fond of Jo-Jo and, although I knew I didn't have any evidence to support it, I feared that she fancied Rex and that Rex fancied her and maybe that's why she and Steve had split up. Perhaps it was just my wild imagination, but it certainly would account for her giving me daggers this morning in the shop.

'So,' he said, changing the subject, 'are you going to come to this party tonight or what?'

'Well, um, you know – I'd love to but I'm not sure what my, er, my friends are up to,' I stammered, lying on my back and attempting to float so he couldn't see my face.

'Bring them! They're welcome to come.'

'Thanks,' I said, wishing I really could bring them, but knowing it would just be impossible now. I couldn't run the risk of them blurting out my real age and making me look a total idiot. 'I'll ask them.'

'Good,' he said, adding, 'I really want you to be there.'

I didn't mean to lie, especially since something about just being near him made me want to tell him the truth about everything I had ever known. I was too frightened he'd look at me in horror if I told him the truth and discard me like a nectarine stone. Each moment had been too perfect to risk it all with the truth, even if I did feel I might suddenly be stuck down by freak lightning for lying.

As I feared, we eventually got round to the whole age subject. He asked me when my birthday was, and I told him it was in a few weeks' time, and he asked if it was a special one like my twenty-first or something. I kind of scoffed and said, 'Oh, no', as if I was, like, way over the whole twenty-one thing, and he said, 'Well, you can only be about twenty-two at most anyway.' I stuck my nose in the air in mock horror and told him that a *real* gentleman never asks a *real* lady her *real* age – he laughed at me a little and we said no more about it, which only supported my theory that he really was a gentleman of the highest order.

'Age is just a number anyway,' he said, shrugging his shoulders. 'I don't judge people on how *long* they've lived, but *how* they've lived.'

'I couldn't agree more,' I said, smiling at his profoundness and feeling not just a little relieved that he'd said it.

We let the sun dry our wet bodies back at the cave and watched the waves lap gently along the shore as we munched on the fruit and cheese. Afterwards, Rex did some spectacular dives off the face of a small cliff and I watched, mesmerised, and clapped my hands excitedly as his perfectly lithe brown body hit the water, making a splash.

'You were right,' I said. 'You're an amazing diver.'

He smiled a little coyly, which made me want to kiss him.

'Well, when you live out here, you spend so much time in the sea it all becomes second nature.'

'Still, it was pretty impressive,' I said, raising my eyebrows.

Afterwards, he sat down next to me closely – *really* closely – and I could smell the scent of the sea and suntan lotion on his skin. I wondered if life got any better than this, just me and him, our bodies almost touching, listening to the sound of the sea in the distance – although I had to admit that a kiss would've been the icing on the cake. Then, just as I was kind of zoning out on my own thoughts, this little butterfly came from nowhere and landed on my knee.

'Don't move!' Rex whispered. And I froze as we both

marvelled at its small furry body and delicate colourful wings shining in the sunlight as they gently opened and closed.

'Buddhists believe that nothing ever truly dies,' Rex said, transfixed by the butterfly. 'And that death simply transports us into another state of being, like the way this little dude was once a caterpillar, and probably something else before it.' He smiled as we watched the butterfly's iridescent wings gently flutter in the light breeze.

I couldn't help but wonder, if this theory were true, then maybe, just maybe, my dad had turned into something else when he had died, and that perhaps, absurd as it was to think, he had returned to the living world as this little butterfly that was sitting on my knee here, to give me his blessing about Rex, to say that it was OK that I had lied and that he was watching over me to make sure I was safe and happy and not to worry about anything. I knew it was a ridiculous thing to think, but it was comforting, just for a second, to believe it.

'I think I'd like to come back as a butterfly,' I said after a few moments, 'because, well, they're beautiful.' And then it fluttered off and we watched it disappear until it was just a tiny dot in the distance.

He smiled at me warmly, our faces closer together now. 'You're as beautiful as a butterfly,' he whispered, which could have been really corny coming from anyone else, but from him it sounded perfect. With his sandy hands he brushed away a few strands of my frizz-ball hair that was in my face, and his lips touched mine. And he tasted sweet. As sweet as the grapes he had brought to eat.

Chapter 8

'How was it?' Ellie asked, as I burst into the apartment. She was sitting down at the table, bits of cotton wool stuck between her toes as she painted them.

'How was what?'

'Duh, the beach, dummy!' she said, pulling a face.

I thought for a second. I wanted to tell her that it had been the most magical moment of my life so far, and that I had wanted to bottle the afternoon like perfume and spray myself all over with it so it would forever linger on my skin, sweet-smelling like coconut, but I thought that would probably sound a bit over the top and she might get suspicious, so I just said, 'Yeah, it was cool, thanks.'

'Mum phoned,' she said, without looking up. 'We had a good chat and she was sorry to have missed you. She sends her love and says she hopes you're having a fabulous time and not to kiss any strange boys.'

I almost started to laugh, because she had no idea how close to the truth she was, although I didn't consider Rex to be either strange nor a boy exactly.

'Did she say she'd ring back?'

'In the next day or so,' answered Ellie, beginning to blow air on her toes to help dry the polish.

'Cool.'

I casually walked into our bedroom, then threw myself down on the bed and clutched the pillow to my face to drown out the squeals of excitement that I could no longer contain. Rex had kissed me again when we had said goodbye outside the lilo shop, and it was just as nice as the first kiss, if not better. 'I don't want to be the one to have to say goodbye first,' I had said to him. In fact, I hadn't wanted to say goodbye at all. 'Well, I'll say goodbye first,' he said. And he stood there. 'Goodbye first, Izzy.'

'Goodbye second, Rex,' I said, and he had kissed me again.

He'd made me promise to ring him because he said he was old-fashioned and hated 'all that texting malarkey'. With that reminder, I actually managed to buy the phone credit I had originally gone to the shop for earlier.

Rex had also made me promise to come along to Café Del Sol that night and I'd told him I would really try, because the thought of not seeing him for more than a few hours suddenly made me want to wither up and die like a plant that someone had forgotten to water.

I wanted to relive the afternoon over and over. But as hard as I tried to recapture the events – the moped, the cheese and grapes and lassi (which incidentally is a bit like a yoghurt drink), and the butterfly, Rex's daring dives off the face of the small cliff (that I was sure he had done just to try and impress me, which it did, massively), and that kiss, that soft lingering kiss – all that I could think of was how much I had lied through my teeth to Ellie to get there. And the thought of this kept creeping back into my head, threatening to ruin everything.

I rolled over on to my tummy and reached for my mobile that was still in my little rucksack. I brushed the grains of sand that had gathered there back into the bag, because discarding them somehow seemed wrong. I wanted to save them for ever, a souvenir of my perfect day with him.

I had a text message: HOWZ IT GOIN IBIZA QUEEN? R U AVIN IT LRG? W X

It was Willow, of course.

LRGE NOT DA WORD. I AM IN LOVE! IZ X

I pressed 'send' and lay back down on the bed. Almost instantly my phone beeped.

NO WAY! WHO IS HE? W X

I tapped back furiously. A DJ. OWN MOPED. 100% GORGE. IZ X

If that didn't get her to call me, nothing would, and sure enough only a minute or so passed before my phone lit up and I heard that familiar ring tone.

'Can't talk for long, got zero credit and off to the piccies with Chantal now . . .'

'Oh!' I said. 'Who's Chantal?'

'Never mind that! Who is this DJ bloke with his own moped? You little minx!'

'Oh Wils,' I wailed, 'I don't know where to begin . . .'

'Er, try at the beginning,' she said.

And so I did my best to tell her the story of how Rex and I had met, and that he was this twenty-six-year-old DJ with his own moped and house in Es Cana, and that he'd taken me to the beach and fed me grapes, and that he wanted to see me again, but that I hadn't told him how old I really was. Willow had oh-so-casually said, 'Well, just don't tell him, then.' After all, she had pointed out, I was only in Ibiza for three weeks, and in all likelihood I would never see him again, and I should just enjoy having a holiday romance and stop being a stress-head, because it wasn't as if I was going to marry the guy, was it?

'Listen, what he doesn't know can't hurt him,' she said, resolutely. 'Besides, it's about time you had some fun and romance in your life.'

I wished I could be more like Willow. I always managed to over-complicate everything with all my 'what ifs' and major stress-outs about everything.

But she was right. Where *could* it all go? I was here for a three-week holiday and he was here for ever – Ibiza was his home – and eventually I'd have to say goodbye, even though the thought of it already paralysed me with dread.

'You know what, you're right,' I said, suddenly full of determination. 'Maybe I should just go for it and enjoy the moment. I mean, what's the worst that could happen?'

'Atta girl!' Willow said, sounding pleased that I'd taken her advice. 'Anyway, listen babes, got to run, Chantal's waiting for me and I can't be late. I have to hear more about DJ boy though – sorry – *man,*' she said, giggling. 'Call me when you can, Stan,' she said, doing that rhyming thing she sometimes does at the end of sentences. 'And Iz, try not to blow it all by letting that *mahoosive* conscience of yours get the better of you. Just enjoy yourself and have a giggle. It's only three weeks, and just think how you can make Toby Parker suffer by blabbing about this *faaabulous* superstar DJ with a moped you snogged while you were in Ibiza . . .'

'OK, I'll let you know how it all goes,' I promised.

'Defo. And get a tan for me *pleeeeease!*' she giggled.

'Love you, Wils,' I said.

'You too, Barney Magoo,' she said, adding, 'Twenty-six! Can you believe it? *You lucky cow!*' before she hung up.

I momentarily thought about our conversation and this Chantal girl and how it had sounded a bit like Wils had wanted to get off the phone to meet her. I wondered if I was just being paranoid, because I'd only been gone a few days and surely Wils wouldn't have suddenly found a new best friend in that time, would she? I didn't have too long to dwell on it though because suddenly Ellie burst in the room.

'Don't bother knocking,' I said sarcastically. 'I could've been naked.'

'I won't and you aren't,' she shot back. 'Listen you've got less than an hour to get ready and then we're going to La Tropicana for dinner, so get a move on, lazy arse.'

I saw the others through the door; they were all looking at a magazine and pointing to something and laughing.

'Actually, Els, I feel a bit sick,' I said, clutching my stomach and feigning illness. 'I think it must be something I ate.' I had to try and convince her to go out with her friends without me. It was my only hope of getting to meet him. I knew they were planning to go to Galaxy, this 'superclub' on the other side of the island, and this was perfect. It was too far away to worry about her popping back to check if I was OK.

I made some soft groaning sounds. 'I might stay here tonight if that's cool. Look, you go. It would be mental to miss out on my account. I know you promised Mum you'd take care of me and everything, but I really don't mind being here on my own,' I said, adding another sharp 'ohhh' sound for authenticity. 'I've got my CDs and magazines, and Edie and her parents are just a few apartments down the block so I could always go there in an emergency,' I said, quickly adding, 'not that there'll be one.' Ellie opened her mouth to speak, but I continued. 'I promise not to open the door to anyone and I'll keep my mobile on. Really, it'll all be fine. You just go and have a great time. I'll be better by tomorrow I'm sure.' I pulled my knees up to my chest and put my arms around my legs. Ellie gave me a look that fell somewhere between concern and gratitude, although I could see she was at pains to hide the latter. She sat down on the bed next to me. Her clear skin was glowing and her pink dress set off the tan she'd miraculously somehow already managed to acquire in, like, two days, and in that second I felt a wave of love for her. I knew in my heart that she only wanted what was best for me. I wanted to reach out to her and tell her I was so happy yet frightened because I had met someone that had made me feel different about myself, and I was scared and excited, and could she help me.

'You really feel that bad?' Ellie said, placing her hand on my brow to check for a temperature.

'Yes,' I croaked, pathetically. 'I mean, I'm sure I'll be OK if I get some rest tonight though.'

Ellie continued to stare at my face, surveying it carefully like she was checking for any notable changes.

'Are you sure you're happy with this?' she said after what seemed like minutes, but was probably just seconds. 'I mean, me going out with the others and leaving you here?'

'Honestly Els,' I said, 'don't feel bad, just go and have a good time. I'll be perfectly OK. Remember I'm sixteen, not six.'

Ellie was quiet for a few seconds and then said, 'If you get worse, you must promise to call me and I'll come back straight away.'

'Yes,' I said.

'Promise,' Ellie demanded.

'I promise, straight away,' I said.

'Right then,' she said sharply, signifying the end of the conversation. 'I'd better get going.'

Ellie stood up and smoothed down her dress.

I looked at her, a tall svelte vision in pink; her glossy caramel-highlighted hair cascading past her shoulders and hanging in perfect strands, her killer cleavage that subconsciously drew your eye to it, and her smooth tanned legs that just seemed to go on for ever.

'You look so pretty,' I said, my voice dry and cracking, and I really did sound sick this time, genuinely so.

'Thanks Iz,' she said, smiling softly at me now, and I felt a little bit better.

'Oh, and Els,' I said, just as she was closing the door behind her. 'What does "self-deprecating" mean?'

Chapter 9

The stretch of sand in front of Café Del Sol was already buzzing with people. I was amazed I'd managed to find my way there as Rex had only explained the directions to me briefly when we'd said our goodbyes earlier and I'd been too busy thinking about our kiss to properly concentrate on what he'd been saying. As it was, though, I found my way without even having to stop and ask anyone, which made me think that Rex and I had this subconscious telepathic thing going on between us that they say people in love can sometimes have. At least that's what I wanted to believe.

Girls and guys were scattered around the rocks that surrounded the small area of beach in front of Café Del Sol enjoying the last moments of the day's fading sunshine. The atmosphere was relaxed, yet full of promise of what the rest of the night had in store. Soft, ambient music filled the warm air as everyone got into the pre-clubbing party spirit. I wondered if I might spot some people from Alfredo's party and if so, would they tell Ellie that they'd bumped into me? *This lying business is extremely stressful,* I thought to myself, *so many things to think about and tracks to cover.* No wonder I was on edge.

Café Del Sol had a huge patio which led right out on to the beach and I could see the bar staff inside busily fixing drinks, their heads bobbing up and down to the gentle sound of the beats. I stood a little way back from the scene and composed myself.

He'd said to meet him there at eight when I had called him earlier, and I was bang on time again because Mum had always said that being prompt would stand me in good stead in life – and I hoped that this included my love life too. He'd sounded happy on the phone, dead chatty and friendly, which was so different to the one-word grunts and awkward silences that I was used to with the lads I'd known back home. He had talked about our day together and how he'd stopped off to buy some fresh olives from this farmer on his way home. I'd said they sounded delicious, the olives, even though I didn't much like them – Willow and I were forever picking them off our pizzas in disgust – but Rex had this way of making everything sound so fantastic that I found myself saying I'd like to try them.

I looked around me at the throngs of clubbers and tried to spot Rex in amongst them. And then this guy suddenly came up behind me from nowhere.

'Fancy coming to a club later, gorgeous?' he asked, handing me a flyer that had *Love in Paradise* written on it. 'You should come along; we could do with a higher babe count.' I smiled politely, which must've made him think I was interested in talking to him, because he came towards me and put his arm around my waist and started blathering on about this party. It was such a relief to see Rex walking towards us, even though I was a bit worried about what he might think, me standing there with some other lad's arm round my waist.

'Hey, Davey, get your hands off my woman!' Rex said, although I could tell he wasn't angry because he was smiling.

'Sorry, Rex, didn't know she was taken,' the guy smiled back, cheekily.

It felt good that he'd referred to me as 'my woman' and I suddenly had this urge to run into his arms and hug him.

'Don't mind Davey.' Rex smiled apologetically when the guy sloped off. 'He's always trying it on. Not that I can blame him – just look at you! You look ... you look stunning, Iz, really stunning.' I was wearing a white strapless dress that I'd pinched from Ellie's case, so I had to be careful not to spill anything down it. Yet another thing to worry about.

'Thanks.' I smiled broadly, hoping I didn't have any lipstick on my teeth.

'Come on,' he said, 'I want you to meet some friends of mine.'

So he introduced me to Steve 'The Spin Doctor' Jones, his DJ buddy and the one he lived with in Es Cana, and he was dead friendly and sweet and told me I looked 'super foxy', which made me feel even more amazing, even if I did think he was probably just trying to be nice. Then he introduced me to Clare and Chloe, two blonde girls that were standing around drinking and laughing and looking glamorous.

'So where you from then?' Chloe asked, smiling at me in a friendly way.

'London,' I replied coolly, desperately trying to hide my nerves.

'Wicked place,' Chloe nodded, smiling. 'Been there twice. Clubs are ace.'

'You working out here for the summer then?' asked Clare.

'Just here on holiday,' I replied with a tentative smile, hoping I was being interesting enough.

'We're out here for the season; doing a bit of PR work for some clubs, handing out flyers and stuff. It's been well heavy.' Which I took to mean as 'good'.

'How do you know Rex?' asked Chloe, casually.

'We met at Alfredo's party. Alfredo's this guy who holds these amazing par—'

'I know who he is,' Chloe said interrupting, although her tone was still light.

I felt stupid. Of course she knew. She was one of the clubbing elite.

'How do you know Rex?' I asked, unable to help myself.

'*Everyone* knows Rex,' Chloe smiled. 'He's a great guy – totally genuine. You'll have fun with him.'

I smiled at them and nodded. *Fun.* Was that all it would be? I couldn't help but think, *hope*, it might be more than that. But I had to get real. It would probably just be a holiday romance, over just as soon as it had started. I remembered my pledge to stay away from lads until I could be sure about not getting hurt, but I just couldn't stop myself wanting to find out what would happen between us. With Rex, my heart had completely overruled my head and I was powerless to stop it.

Chloe and Clare asked me what I did for a living and I told them I was studying to be a vet, which led them to enquire which university I was at and, before I could make up yet another damned lie, Jo-Jo turned up and inadvertently saved me. She looked totally stunning as ever in this black catsuit type thing that showed off her cleavage and long legs, and she was wearing her long blond hair up in a high ponytail, and I could tell, just by the other girls' reactions, that the party clearly doesn't start until Jo-Jo arrives.

'Ladies,' she said, acknowledging them like a queen does her courtiers. 'Steve.' She nodded frostily in his direction. 'Hi, Rex,' she said, much more warmly, I noted.

'Hey, Jo,' Rex said, and I was sure he slightly dropped his arm from my waist a bit. 'You good?'

'Uh-huh. Hi, erm – Lizzy isn't it?'

'Izzy,' I said, feeling slightly embarrassed and beginning to worry about the whole arm-dropping thing.

She ignored me. 'You coming up to Adam's Temple later, Rexy?' she said, and I noticed she was looking right at him, her eyes sparkling from the make-up she had on.

Rexy?

'I don't think so, Jo,' he said, apologetically, shooting Steve a sideways look.

'I'm – well, I'm here with . . .' Rex's arm was round me again now, which as you can imagine, was more than a bit of a relief.

'It's cool,' I said, looking up at Rex and feeling compelled to butt in. 'If you fancy going up there later, then no worries.' But Rex said nothing and the four of us stood there all looking

77

at each other in this weird, uncomfortable sort of silence.

'Suit yourself,' said Jo-Jo, sticking her nose in the air as she strode off, her long ponytail swishing behind her.

'You two need to do some serious talking,' Rex said finally as he turned towards Steve, but Steve just shrugged and carried on mixing up some tunes.

'Come on, Iz, let's go and get a drink and watch that sunset.'

The sun was beginning to set, signifying the end to what had so far been the most amazing day of my life. Not even the appearance of Jo-Jo, who I was fast beginning to think hated me, could cast a dark cloud over it.

We had moved away from the revellers now and over to a small part of the beach that was sheltered by rocks.

'Don't worry about Jo-Jo,' Rex said. 'She's just in a mood about her and Steve. Take no notice. She's really quite nice once you get to know her.'

Maybe, I thought.

I looked out towards the sky as the sun began to disappear behind the horizon, casting a rich deep-orange shadow and causing a stream of light to make a path across the sea that looked so beautiful I felt as though I could almost walk across it – although not in these heels, obviously.

'You could have gone to Adam's Temple with her,' I said, adding, 'I wouldn't have minded. I'd only have cried for, ooh, maybe two days.'

I gave him a playful smile and he smiled back as he pulled me towards him.

'Only two days, huh?' he said, his body up close to mine. 'Besides, why would I want to go to Adam's Temple when I have everything I want right here?'

'Oh yeah?' I said, cocking my head to one side, mimicking him. 'And what's that then?'

We were flirting madly and I was totally swept away by it. I couldn't understand where my words were coming from; it was me saying them, that much I knew, but their confidence and self-assurance startled me. It was like I had been taken over by a more cocksure, sassy version of myself, and it scared and excited me in equal measures.

'Oh, you know,' he said, linking his arms round my waist. We were moving together now almost in time to the soft sound of the beats in the distance. 'Well, I've got the best tunes . . . the balmy summer evening on the beach,' he said, gesturing around him, 'and the superbly sublime company of . . .' he let the word hang in the air, poignantly as he looked directly into my eyes, 'Steve,' he said, laughing.

'Pah!' I replied dramatically, and I began to look over his shoulder, as if I was searching for something or *someone.* 'Now, what was that lad's name again? Davey, wasn't it?' I giggled, teasing him back.

'Oi, cheeky, don't even think about it!' he said, laughing with me as we stumbled a little across the sand, refusing to let go of each other.

'Speaking of names,' I said, 'last night at Alfredo's villa, you knew my name before I'd even told you what it was.'

'A-ha!' Rex said. 'There's a simple explanation.'

'And . . .' I said, eager for him to continue.

'I'm telepathic, you see.'

'I knew that already,' I said, giggling.

'You did? How?' he asked, looking at me quizzically.

'Because I'm telepathic too!' I said, unable to keep a straight face.

He threw his head back and laughed a little.

'I had a really amazing day today,' he said more seriously now. I saw a flicker of something in his eyes, but I couldn't put my finger on what it was.

'Me too,' I responded, my heart beginning to stomp in time with the waves that were gently but methodically lapping against the shore.

'Is it something you do a lot? Take girls to the beach and feed them cheese and grapes?' I was careful to ask in a jokey way so as not to make it sound like I doubted him too much. It was unlike me to be so frank, but I just had to know where all this was heading. The brief conversation I'd had with Chloe and Clare made me wonder if I was just another in a long line of girls before me. 'You'll have *fun*.' Fun was good, don't get me wrong, but I was falling for him so fast and with such strength and intensity that it terrified me. I was frightened of getting hurt, of feeling more for him than he would for me. If fun was all it would be, did I really want to get even more deeply involved than I was already?

Rex looked at me strangely, almost as if he had been waiting for me to ask the question.

'I get to meet a lot of girls out here, professional hazard

and all that,' he said, his jokey tone only just detectable now, 'but I've never taken anyone to Cala Jondal before.'

'Really?' I was intrigued, not to mention thrilled.

'Really. That cave is a personal little spot of mine.' He was looking at me intensely, as if trying to bring the point home.

'If you're asking whether I've had girlfriends before, then the answer is yes, of course.'

'No, no,' I said quickly, 'I wasn't . . .' Oh God, now he thought I was some kind of possessive bunny-boiler.

'There's not been anyone special for a long time though. Not until now.'

I felt my heart flip over in my chest. *I* was special?

'And you?' he asked, raising an eyebrow. 'When was the last time you went to the beach with a guy and kissed him?'

I felt myself flush with embarrassment. He was turning the conversation around on me.

'Never,' I said. I wasn't lying either.

He moved in closer towards me and our faces were lightly touching now, nose to nose, and I could feel his warm breath on my cheek and the faint scent of his soapy aftershave.

'This is going to sound really cheesy and crap,' he said.

'Go on . . .'

'Well, I feel as though I've known you for a long time already,' he said. 'Does that make sense, because you know, well, I haven't felt that with anyone for what feels like for ever . . .'

I clung to him and he squeezed me tightly in his arms.

I felt a rush of something course through my body, but I couldn't tell you what it was or even if it had a name. All I knew was that I had never felt anything like it before. It was so powerful and intoxicating that it made the hairs on my neck and arms stand to attention, and I had this sudden urge to run with him, fully-clothed into the sea.

I knew he could be lying to me about not having met anyone special in a long time. After all, I was lying to him about my age – what was stopping him lying to me? Yet somehow, somewhere deep inside me, I believed him. When he had kissed me it was as if I could see right into his soul. I had seen honesty and kindness, and it had felt so real, like I could almost touch it.

'Me neither,' I finally managed to say in response, and there was a conviction in my voice that I'd never heard before and it startled me, especially since when I said 'neither' what I really meant was 'ever'.

We stood there momentarily, just holding each other, looking deeply into each other's eyes. The waves were washing over our feet now and I could feel myself softly sinking into the sand. Neither of us moved. We didn't care. If we were going to sink, we would sink together.

'This is no holiday romance, is it?' Rex breathed quietly after a moment.

'No, I don't think it is,' I whispered back, biting my lip nervously. I closed my eyes as his lips found mine, hungry and passionate. And we lost ourselves in each other as we kissed for what felt like an eternity.

I'd read about these moments in books and seen them

in films, that singular, spectacular moment where two people fall in love. I had hoped for a 'thunderbolt' moment all my life. Willow always said I was a hopeless romantic (which so far had proved true, in as much as all the romances in my life so far had been hopeless) because I had dreamed of it since I was a little girl – how I'd meet that special person and how he would sweep me off my feet and I would love him for ever.

And here it was. I had thought I could fall in love with Rex from the moment I laid eyes on him. Then on our first date under the backdrop of the sun and pine trees I had had an inkling it *might* be love. Now, from the depths of my heart to the core of my very being, I felt sure that it really was. An all-consuming, burning desire had taken over me: there, on the beach, holding each other, the soft, tranquil waves washing over our toes as we moved in unison. As he held me, something inside me had let go. I was nervous, like I always was in any romantic situation, but this was a new kind of fear. The type of fear I imagined actors might get before they go on stage to give the performance of a lifetime, paralysed with terror, but exhilarated and driven by the standing ovation that would rightfully be theirs at the final curtain. In that moment with Rex everything in my life had come right. All my awkwardness and inhibitions abandoned me, leaving this newly confident person in their place. It was as if I had been unzipped and had stepped out of myself, shedding the old Izzy to make way for the new one. Like I'd been born again.

Chapter 10

I t was the following evening, and Cala Jondal looked
different in the shade of the night: empty with only the
moonlight to guide us and the gentle lapping of the
waves – but it was no less beautiful, in fact, it was even more
peaceful and tranquil than it had been in the heat of the
midday sun.

After a dinner of fresh paella, Ellie and Co. had decided
to go to a little gathering that Alfredo was organising down
at Playa d'en Bossa beach, and I had said that I was too tired
to join them owing to my recent 'illness'. Ellie hadn't
questioned this, but had made me promise to text when I got
back to the apartment, and I'd said I would. I knew they
would be gone for the duration of the night but I still had to
play it carefully if I was to meet Rex and get away with it –
again.

Rex had been doing his usual slot at Café Del Sol and
after his set he had whisked me off on his moped, saying
he wanted to take me somewhere. I was a bit surprised
when I realised he had brought me back to the beach. *Our*
beach.

'You didn't have to cut your set short, you know,' I
said, worried in case he'd done it on my account.

'I really wanted to bring you here again because, well,
yesterday felt so good and everything, but you know I

wasn't sure if you'd think, well, that I was trying to get you alone, in the dark, and you know . . .'

'And are you?' I said, raising my eyebrows in a half jokey, half worried way.

'No!' he shot back, quickly. 'Well, yes, but no, not because of *that* . . .'

He looked as amazing as ever, his glossy honey-coloured hair falling down by his broad shoulders, and the stripy shirt he was wearing set off his deep golden tan and made his emerald eyes shine. I noticed he was wearing those little beads again and I finally remembered to ask him about them.

'These?' he said, putting his hand up to his neck. 'Well, there's a story behind them . . .'

'Now how did I know that?' I giggled, putting my knees up to my chest to get comfortable.

'Up in Es Cana, you know, where I live, there's this hippy market – I think I told you about it?' he said, checking my expression for confirmation. 'Anyway, there's this guy, Juan Pablo, and he's just the most amazing dude ever – this real hippy from the Sixties, not one of those wannabe hippies who're everywhere now, selling their mass-produced tat while banging on about the evils of capitalism, but the real deal.' He ruffled his hair with one hand and continued. 'Well, he lives in an old van-type mobile home with no running water or electricity or anything. He thinks television is to blame for all the evil in the world, which when you think about it probably has some truth in it, and he makes his own fires and eats off the land by catching fish from the sea and picking fruit and olives and stuff. Anyway, I kind of met him by accident one time when I was on my way back from the market – he sells some of his jewellery there that he makes himself – and he ran after me, saying that these beads had spoken to him. Apparently, they'd called out to him and said that I must have them and that they would bring me luck and keep me safe from harm. I've never taken them off since.'

'They *spoke* to him?' I asked, intrigued.

'Yeah, although I don't think he meant it literally, because hey, I don't think beads can talk, can they?' He laughed and I giggled too.

'He said that as I had walked past him, the beads began to tingle in his fingers, and he said it was a sign that they were destined to belong to me, which I thought was kind of cool.'

'That's amazing,' I said, wishing I had some talking beads too, to bring me luck.

'I hang out with him sometimes. We fish together and build fires and occasionally I help him thread some of his beads to sell . . .'

'And he still lives in this van?' I asked, genuinely interested.

'Yeah. No water, no telly, nothing . . .'

'Wow. No TV,' I said and I tried to imagine what my life would be like without any soaps or reality TV or music channels, and I shuddered a bit.

'I don't watch TV,' Rex said casually, as if it were the most normal thing to say in the world.

'What, ever?' I asked, trying not to sound too freaked out.

'Not any more. There's too much natural beauty here to be a cabbage in front of a telly. I'm always out and about DJing, having fun, living in the real world instead of watching fictional people living their lives in one that isn't.'

I had to admit that putting it like that made total sense.

'I read the papers, keep up with what's going on in the world, and sometimes I'll have a look on the Internet – I e-mail my folks quite a bit.'

I was glad he didn't mind e-mail because he didn't much like texting and I wondered if he would keep in touch with me via e-mail when I was back home. And then I realised I had thought about home, of being without him. It made me seriously panic, so I tried to concentrate on sitting next to him right now and not worry about it. Only I couldn't stop myself thinking about leaving him, thoughts of those final moments kept breaking through the barriers in my mind and torturing me.

It was all so unfair. Why couldn't we have met in London, or at the very least, England, where there wouldn't be so much distance between us? Why did there always have to be a goodbye? Hadn't I said goodbye to enough people I loved already? Just when something as momentous as falling in love happens to me, it would be ruthlessly cut short. I would board a plane and it would all be gone and I'd be back to being plain old Izzy.

'Sometimes it's difficult to live in the moment,' I thought and then I realised I'd said this out loud.

'Yeah it is, isn't it?' he said, turning to face me, and I was so relieved that he'd agreed and not looked at me like I was some kind of loony-toon, because what I'd said didn't have much to do with what he'd been talking about.

'Everyone talks about living in the past and always looking to the future, but no one really talks about the here and now.'

I really wasn't sure where all this profound stuff was coming from, or that it was coming out of my mouth at all.

'You're so right . . .' he said, his voice trailing off.

'Not that the past or future aren't important,' I continued, on a roll now. 'Although I have to confess,' I said, 'sometimes the here and now does involve watching a bit of telly.' I tried to keep a straight face, but it didn't last long.

'You know what the best thing about the here and now is?' he said, when we'd finally stopped laughing.

'No. What?' I asked, lowering my eyes provocatively. I was flirting – like, *badly* flirting.

'You,' he said, and he leaned in closer and put his arms around my neck and he kissed me tenderly, and my lips tingled too, just like Juan Pablo's beads.

* * *

After walking along the sand, hand in hand, for a while, Rex suggested we lie down and look up at the stars, because that's why he'd brought me here after all.

'If we wait long enough we might see a shooting star – I've seen lots of them this summer,' he said. So we both lay there, still and silent, hoping we might catch one. But nothing happened and eventually I quietly said, 'My mum reckons my dad is a star.'

'Your dad?' he asked, puzzled.

'Yeah, after he died, that's what she told me he'd become, although since recent events I'm beginning to think he might really be a butterfly.'

Rex sat up and crossed his legs.

'Oh Iz, I'm sorry. I didn't know your dad was . . .'

'Dead,' I said, finishing his sentence, because I was used to people not being able to actually say *that* word.

'Do you want to talk about it?'

I thought for a moment and then said that yes, I did. It had been so long since I had spoken to anyone about my dad. It was coming up to the anniversary of the day it had happened, and I always thought about it all so much more around this time – in fact, I mostly thought about nothing else.

I had never spoken about the events of that day, the day my dad was taken from me. I'd not even told Willow all the details, unable to bring myself to repeat them in case I would suddenly be transported right back to that very moment and have to relive the agony all over again. Until now I had kept my thoughts buried deep inside me, locked in a cage around my heart, and sometimes the sheer weight of them pulled me down. Now, more than ever, I felt as though I needed to speak about it, to unlock some of the grief that was constantly bubbling under the surface, forever threatening to erupt from me like an angry volcano.

It seemed somehow right to tell Rex. Just being near

him made me want to tell him my feelings, explain all I knew and felt inside about everything. It was almost instinctive. I trusted him. I knew it was crazy. In the grand scheme of things, we'd only just met. Yet despite this, it was as if he had found a window into my heart and opened it, letting out the stuffy contents, allowing fresh air into my soul. He made me want to open up to him and show him who I really was. I knew that telling him about my dad was the biggest step I'd ever taken with anyone, let alone someone I'd only known a matter of days. But just so long as I was with him, I sensed all would be well.

The worst, most hideous, thing of all though was that I knew I would have to lie again, explain that it had all happened coming up for twelve years ago instead of the six that it really was, so as not to give my age away. And this felt all the more bitterly deceitful, because when it came to my dad, I never wanted to speak anything but the truth. I knew that now was not the right time to break the whole age thing to Rex, though. Even so, this lie, told to support the other, burned deeper than ever and filled me with an abhorrent self-loathing.

As we lay there together, side by side in the sand, our bodies gently touching, I began to tell him about that day and how my dad had been hit by a car while crossing the road on his way home. It had been a few days short of my eleventh birthday, and he was carrying presents that he'd bought for me in his arms when the car crashed into him. I told Rex about the witnesses who'd said he didn't stand a chance, because the car was just going so fast and everything. I imagined how the presents must've looked, all battered and broken lying in the road – just like him. I talked about how the paramedics had tried to resuscitate him on the pavement and how they really tried hard for, like, twenty minutes or so, but you know, he was gone, just like that. I told him how I vividly recalled standing behind my mum at the door when the police came, because I thought it might be my dad coming home and that I'd catch him with my presents and that maybe he'd let me have one of them early, because my dad was like that. A real soft touch, and my mum always said I could wrap him round my little finger. And I didn't really know why my mum was crying so much because the police were talking with her in hushed, muffled voices so I didn't really hear what they were saying. I sensed something terrible had happened, though, by the way she almost collapsed and had to be helped to the armchair by a policewoman.

I could feel my eyes welling up with tears as I was speaking and I tried not to blink so as to stop them from falling down my face.

'They gave my mum the presents you know. My birthday presents...' I said, my voice cracking. 'They picked them all up off the street and gave them to her all smashed and broken and torn – except for this one thing; this perfect little pink jewellery box with a ballerina inside that turned round and round and played a twinkly tune from the *Nutcracker Suite*. It was completely untouched, not a scratch on it – and even though I didn't celebrate my birthday that year, because, well, there was nothing to celebrate, my mum gave me the little box with the ballerina inside. I just sat there for hours and hours playing it over and over again until I thought it might break. Sometimes now I wake up in the night and hear that tune. I wonder if Dad knows I'm thinking of him and that I love him. Then I wonder if I really do love him or if I just love the memory of him because how can you love someone that doesn't exist any more? And then I feel guilty and . . . and . . .'

But it was no good. Warm wet tears began rolling down the sides of my face and trickling into my ears as I lay there and I had this dull ache in my chest that stopped me from breathing properly. Wretched sobs escaped from my mouth and although I was now crying uncontrollably, it felt strangely therapeutic to talk about my dad and to finally let it all out.

Rex had listened, just as I thought he would. He didn't say anything. He just held me tightly and wiped away my tears as they made tracks down the sides of my face.

'You know just because someone isn't there any more, doesn't mean that we ever stop loving them,' he said gently, as he pulled me closer into his arms then stroked my face tenderly. And he felt warm, warm and strong and protective, and it helped. It helped so much.

Chapter 11

I t was Friday, six days since our arrival in Ibiza and the longest period of time I had ever gone without speaking to my mum. So when she called, I felt a strange kind of relief, like things would be OK and normal again, even though I felt sure that as soon as I opened my mouth she would hear that something in me had changed. My mum has this sixth sense of knowing when something is up with me, so I was naturally a bit wary when I took the mobile phone from my sister. Ellie had been chatting to Mum for over fifteen minutes – in private, I had (somewhat worryingly) noticed. I slipped out on to the balcony and slid the door shut behind me. If Ellie could have a private chat with our mum then so could I.

'Hello, rabbit. Ellie tells me you're having a ball,' Mum said, sounding excited and happy for us. I could hear our cat, Montague, purring in the background.

'Yeah, it's great here, Mum,' I replied, trying my best to sound normal, even though I felt anything but. 'The island is so beautiful and the beaches are great and everything . . .'

'I'm so glad you're having a good time, although I've really missed my girls; the house has felt so empty without you.' She sounded a bit sad and I immediately felt bad, because the last time I recall my mum saying something similar was when Dad had died.

'Bet you're glad of the peace,' I said, trying not to think about it.

'Nonsense, you know I like a full house,' Mum said, and I was sure she was thinking the same thing as I had been.

'Montague, get down . . . Do you want me to record *That Certain Something* for you on Saturday, chickie?' she asked, changing the subject. Missing my favourite reality TV show was the least of my worries and, besides, I wasn't even sure I cared about it much any more, or anything on telly for that matter. The only thing I could think about right now was Rex, and when I would next get to see him, and whether or not I should come clean and confess the truth to him about my age.

'Nah, it's OK, Mum. I reckon I'll survive,' I said.

'Really? But it's the final,' Mum said, sounding a little concerned, and I wondered if I should've just said yes so as not to arouse any suspicion.

'I saw Willow in town yesterday,' she said, casually changing the subject. 'She was with a girl friend but I didn't go over and say hello because they looked like they were deep in conversation and I didn't think they'd want an oldie like me interrupting them.'

'Oh,' I said, instantly worried that the 'girl friend' she was referring to was this Chantal that Wils had been spending loads of time with, doing all the stuff we usually did together, like shopping and watching fit lads.

'Bet you're missing each other madly, seeing as though you two are usually glued together at the hip.' Mum laughed.

'Yeah, I really do miss her,' I said, although I wondered if Willow really was missing me as much as I was missing her, now that she had this new friend.

'I miss you too though, Mum,' I found myself saying.

'Oh, rabbit, I miss you as well,' Mum said, getting a bit sentimental. 'And so does Montague, don't you, Monts?' He purred loudly down the phone.

'Are you sure you're all right, Iz? You sound – well, are you sure everything's OK? Are you and Ellie getting on all right?'

'Yeah, Mum, everything's fine,' I said, and I really hoped it would be. I was just so confused about everything: about Willow and what was happening to our friendship – if indeed anything was happening at all – and about me and Ellie, and the fact that I had been deceiving her in a big way. And then of course there was Rex, who had come into my life from nowhere and turned everything inside out and upside down and back to front. Even though I had fallen in love, my world before Rex, and the relationships I had within that world, seemed as though they were falling apart at the seams.

'Good-o,' Mum said. 'Greg will be picking you up from the airport. I can't make it because I'm off to the hospital with Auntie Maureen that day.'

'Hospital? Is Auntie Maureen sick or something?' I asked, concerned.

'Well, just between you and me, pussy-cat, she's going through some *changes* at the moment and has turned into a worse version of Fang.' Mum laughed loudly.

Fang was this pet rabbit we once had when I was a kid that would bite you if you ever tried to touch him – hence the name.

'I hope you don't mind, poppet. I'll be back before you get home anyway.'

'That's cool, Mum,' I said, wishing I could see her, because suddenly I wanted her to hold me and comfort me, like she had always done since I was small.

'Have you met any boys then?' she asked, brightly. 'Go on, you can tell your old mum!'

'Mum!' I laughed, embarrassed because I didn't really speak to her about boys, mainly because when she had asked me in the past, I didn't have much to tell her. But now I did and I really wanted her advice because she was pretty level-headed. But I knew that even she'd be shocked by my confession about Rex, so I kept my mouth shut.

'No rich millionaires with their own yacht desperate for your hand in marriage then?' she joked.

'No, Mum,' I said, in mock annoyance.

'Pity,' she laughed. 'I was hoping to marry you off to some rich Spaniard so I could get to holiday in Marbella every year, gratis!'

'Fat chance,' I sniffed.

'Ah well, bunny, plenty of time for all that,' she said. 'Gotta dash, Monts is pulling holes in my new bouclé skirt, and I've got to get to QuickShop for cat food and eggs before it shuts. Oh, the glamorous life I lead!' she joked.

'Love you, Mum,' I said quietly, because I realised I didn't tell her enough.

'Love you too, rabbit,' she said, softly.

And when she hung up I started to cry. But I was forced to dry my eyes quickly because, soon after, Louisa began banging on the patio window at me and beckoning me inside.

'It's going to be totally gangsta!' Louisa said, pulling a vast array of brightly-coloured bikinis and sarongs from her case and holding them up for inspection. 'Ellie and Narinda are getting ready in their rooms and Charlie's in the shower, so I need you to help me decide on some suitable beach attire,' she commanded.

I wiped my eyes on the back of my hand and hoped she wouldn't notice I'd been crying. I smiled at her nervously. She was more caustic and abrupt than Narinda and Charlotte and was the only one out of Ellie's gang who I felt quite jittery around.

'So what exactly *is* this champagne-diving party all about then?' I asked adding, 'I gather it probably involves champagne and, er, diving . . .'

'Not bad, Sherlock,' Louisa said, derisively. 'It's like this,' she continued, 'loads of us get on this big boat and bottles of champagne are thrown overboard and everyone has to dive in the sea and retrieve them, ideally before they sink to the bottom. Then after the diving and the food and the free drinks, the whole thing turns into one big party and everyone just goes mental until they drop and the sun comes up again!' She squealed excitedly and began doing this funny little booty-shaking-type dance around the room. 'It's a great way to start the week!'

Don't get me wrong, I was excited about the day's forthcoming events too, even though I knew I should be showing it more. It wasn't just the phonecall with Mum; I knew this was the opportunity of a lifetime, but I would have traded it all in for five minutes with Rex. Last night's conversation had created an unspoken bond between us that I knew could never be broken. I felt even closer to him as a result of opening up to him about Dad. For me to even *want* to do this made me realise how special he was. He had been so kind, so gentle and understanding. I had told him he was a good listener, and he had said that who or whatever had made us had given us *two* ears and *one* tongue, and that people didn't listen to one another enough. And I had thought that it was just so incredible that he always seemed to say the right thing.

By agreeing to accompany Ellie and Co. to today's events I had forfeited spending an evening with him. Not through choice, I add, but because I simply couldn't find a way to get out of it. Ellie had bought five tickets to the boat party and was particularly keen to see my expression when she had handed them out early this morning.

'Don't tell me you've already made plans with that Edie girl, for crying out loud,' Ellie had said to me, almost crossly, before I'd even had the chance to speak. 'These tickets are like gold dust!'

Rex had sounded slightly dejected when I'd said I wouldn't be able to meet him that night. 'My friends have made other plans,' I mumbled weakly to him on the phone. 'I can't really get out of it now and —'

'It's cool, Iz,' he'd interrupted, attempting to sound chirpy. 'I think I'm DJing at Adam's Temple this evening, just thought you might like to be my guest. You can bring your friends, they're welcome to come too.'

'You know I'd really love to and everything but I —'

'Hey, it's no problem, really,' he said softly, his voice suddenly sounding all husky and sexy, 'so long as you're not going off me or anything.' He was only half joking I could tell.

'No, really, it's not that, God, it's not that at all – I . . . I just . . . well, my friend has already bought the tickets.' This was a nightmare. I wished I could suddenly turn to liquid and pour myself down the receiver to where he was, and then turn back into myself again and hold him and kiss him and tell him I loved him. Because I did. Even if I knew it might be too soon to say it and wasn't sure what his reaction would be. The fact was I would've foregone a thousand boat parties, even ones with *real* celebs. I would have forsaken it all just for five minutes in his arms. It had choked me to have to turn him down. And it had worried me too. What if he really *did* think I had gone off him? Surely not? Not since we'd got so close and last night and everything. I closed my eyes, as if somehow it would help me to stop worrying. Falling in love was so amazing, I thought. It had lifted me right up out of myself and given me a lightness of being I had never felt before. But I figured it was because I'd fallen in love that all these irrational insecurities kept creeping in. I was scared and I sensed that maybe even Rex was scared too. Giving your heart to someone means trusting them not to break it.

'Almost ready,' I said to no one in particular half an hour later, daring to take a glimpse of myself in the mirror. I was wearing my red-and-white polka dot bikini, the Fifties style one that I hoped had a Marilyn Monroe vibe about it, and Narinda had lent me one of her kaftans, a beautiful silky red one that had intricate gold beading on the front. I had tied my hair back – as neatly as my hair could go – off my face and put my big sunglasses on and, for a split second, I didn't recognise myself. Was this glam, sophisticated girl I saw in the reflection really me? I almost looked cosmopolitan, like someone else I might see on the beach and admire, even if I did say so myself. I wished so much that Rex could see me now. If he hadn't fallen in love with me already, then surely, once he clapped eyes on me looking like this, he would be powerless not to.

'Stop looking at yourself,' Ellie said, smiling as she caught my eye.

Embarrassed, I felt my face flush bright red and I turned away from the mirror, but Ellie put her hand on my arm and stopped me.

'You look really great, Iz,' she said softly, taking a step back to get a proper look at me. 'Really sophisticated and grown up.'

I stood there, stunned. 'You really think so?' I said, rubbing my lips together to evenly distribute my red lip-gloss, and feeling so chuffed that my chest visibly swelled (which was not such a bad thing, all in all). 'Sophisticated, you say . . .' I turned to the side and began inspecting myself from a different angle in the mirror. 'And grown up . . .' I said aloud, almost forgetting that Ellie was actually still there as I held my nose in the air and flicked my head back like the celebs do on the red carpet when they're posing for photographers. 'No, please, no more photos,' I said, holding my hand up in front of my face, 'have some respect for my privacy; I'm a human being too.' I clutched my chest and put one hand up to cover my face dramatically.

'You,' Ellie said, unable to stifle the amusement on her face, 'are a first class nut-bag, Isabelle Jackson. Now come *on*,' she said. 'If we don't get a move on the boat will leave without us.'

Chapter 12

If I had thought Alfredo's party was full of beautiful people then nothing could have prepared me for the sight I was confronted with as we boarded the imposing party boat. I was surrounded by bikini-clad beauties in what seemed like their hundreds, their bodies lithe and golden and glistening with oil, glossy hair pulled up high in ponytails on their heads or casually hidden underneath super-trendy Stetsons or floppy Sixties straw sunhats. I suddenly felt small and insignificant and nothing like I had done back at the apartment, even after Ellie's unprecedented compliment. The smell of expensive suntan lotion filled the air, making it fragrant and sweet as everyone frantically began to stake their claims on the best sunbeds on the top deck. Needless to say, the first thing Ellie did upon boarding was bag us each a well-positioned lounger.

'Girls,' announced Charlotte, as she provocatively undid her white sarong, allowing it to slip to the floor and expose her bronzed curves, 'let the sunbathing commence!'

Ellie and Narinda wandered off to check out the rest of the boat and get some drinks and left Louisa, Charlotte and me to settle down for an afternoon of catching rays. I reclined on the soft, stripy lounger and involuntarily let out a sigh.

I closed my eyes and tried to relax but it was impossible

for all the thoughts fighting for space in my head. I grappled with my brain, trying to block them out, metaphorically putting my hands over my ears and saying 'la la la, not listening', but I knew that I would have to tell Rex the truth about my age sooner or later. I tried to imagine how he might react. Would he just continue the conversation as if nothing of great note had been said, or would he sit there, open-mouthed in abject horror? *Oh God, I so wish I had just told the truth from the off. It would have been so much easier.* As it was, I was swinging between being utterly convinced that Rex would never have got involved with me in the first place, and then sure that he would see the real me and not care, regardless of how many years I'd spent on the planet. 'Age is just a number anyway . . .' I remembered him saying on our first date. I was hoping his reaction would fall into the latter category, obviously, but the chance that it might not be made me want to lose my lunch over the side of the boat. On top of that, there was something else niggling me. Rex was almost ten years older than me – that much *was* the truth – and even though I had never felt so intensely about anyone in my life before, or more relaxed with anyone, this unnerved me a little. I mean, would we want the same things from life? I felt irked with myself. Why couldn't I just do as Willow had suggested? Just enjoy these three weeks with him and have an amazing time and not worry about the future.

I sat up abruptly. It was time to text Willow. I needed a distraction and, moreover, support.

HEY U. AM ON A PARTY BOAT SUNNING MYSELF + LISTENING 2 TUNES. WOT U UP 2? IZ X

I waited for my phone to beep back. Willow was a super-fast texter who never left her phone out of sight. And seconds later sure enough . . .

NO WAY! AM I JEALUS OR WOT? CHILLIN WIV CHAN. WOTCHIN FRM HERE 2 ETERNITY. HOWZ IT GOIN WIV DA DJ? TELL ALL. W X

I stared at my phone, my eyes blurry from the heat and sun cream. CHILLIN WIV CHAN. WOTCHIN FRM HERE 2 ETERNITY.

How could she? *From Here to Eternity* was *our* film. It was sacred to *us*. I felt a pang of jealousy swiftly followed by hurt.

I poised my fingers to text back, but hesitated. What would I say? I wanted to tell Willow, my best friend in the world, all about the trauma I was facing and the web of lies I had spun. I wanted her help. I needed her to tell me what I should do, what my next move should be, like she had always done. I didn't want some new, unknown girl lingering in the background. I shuddered. *Stop, Izzy, stop it now!*

I had to text back. I didn't want her to think I was blanking her.

I NEED YOUR HELP WITH DJ MAN. I wrote, and then immediately deleted it and tapped out: ALL IS COOL BABES. FINGS GOIN GR8. GETTING A GOOD TAN. NJOY DA FILM. IT'S DA BEST. MISS U LOVE U, IZ X

It was best not to mention anything. I just couldn't deal with it on top of everything else.

I pressed 'send' and fell back on to the sun lounger.

Everything had changed. I'd been in Ibiza less than one week and suddenly I didn't know who I was any more, like the past sixteen – almost seventeen – years had happened to someone else. My friendship with Willow – who had been my rock my whole life, there for me without fail in every love crisis, family crisis, clothes crises and countless hair crisis – that I had valued and treasured all my life suddenly felt fragile and disposable, and it shook me to the core.

Rex was right, I decided. Texting *was* rubbish.

'They're starting to throw the champagne off the boat. C'mon, let's go and see if we can get some.' Ellie and Narinda had returned from the bar laden with a tray of ice-cool drinks. Grateful for the distraction from my thoughts, I sat up and slipped my flip-flops on my feet. 'I'll come and watch,' I said. 'Wait for me.'

'OK,' said the handsome deck guy dressed in white shorts and an equally white T-shirt. 'On the count of three. One . . . two . . . !' We were on the lower deck now, closer to the sea. It was coming towards the end of the afternoon, but the sun was still strong and blazing on my back. A fairly impressive crowd had gathered, waiting for him to throw the first bottle of champagne overboard.

'Go for it, Iz,' Ellie said encouragingly, as I found myself at the front of the gathering crowd. 'You're in a great position.'

'But I can't dive,' I said panicking, looking back at them as more and more people gathered around the front of the boat, putting distance between us.

'Just go for it!' said Charlotte. Narinda, who was

holding Ellie's hand, began shouting, 'Go Izzy, go Izzy!'

'I can't,' I said, gripped with terror. 'I don't like deep water . . . There could be sharks!'

But the pressure was on me now.

'Yeah, you can . . .' Ellie shouted from somewhere behind me. 'You can do it, babes.'

The force of the gathering crowd was almost pushing me overboard and my heart was in my mouth. I daren't look down. There was no way I was going to dive. After all, this was the only girl in the whole of her junior school who didn't manage to dive down to the bottom of a three-metre-deep swimming pool and retrieve the brick in her pyjamas, for God's sake, let alone jump into the abyss surrounding us for a bottle of bubbly, watched by a bunch of Ibiza's elite. How had I ended up in this mess?

It was just as I was thinking this that I saw him. He was on the top deck of the boat chatting to someone: a girl. Yes, it was Jo-Jo. I could see her now, resplendent in a shiny green bikini and matching sun hat, and Steve, his best mate, was on the other side of her. Rex was shirtless, dressed only in baggy denim shorts with a thick leather belt around his waist. He looked tanned and strong and his brown skin was shining in the heat of the sun. Had he seen me? *Could* he see me? I ducked down slightly in among the crowds of spectators and would-be divers, relieved of their shelter. What the hell was he doing here anyway? He hadn't mentioned any boat party to me on the phone, but then again, I realised, neither had I.

'Three!' bellowed the guy in the white shorts. And I

dived – well more panic-jumped than anything, before he could quite finish the final 'e'. I held my breath while pinching my nose tightly and tried to think of dolphins as I hit the cold water.

Of course, I didn't manage to actually grasp the bottle of champagne. I was too busy trying to stay alive. I scrambled back up the rope ladder to the safety of the boat to the cheers and whoops of a delighted Ellie and Co.

'You're one brave girl,' Narinda said, as she helped me up the last rung of the wobbly ladder.

'Way to go, Iz,' Ellie said, handing me a towel to dry myself with. 'You nearly did it. You were only centimetres away from the bottle. 'Come on, let's buy some champagne anyway.'

A bottle of bubbly later, Ellie and gang were getting well into the party spirit. I on the other hand, was gripped in a nightmare of unadulterated fear and panic. *I had seen him, here on the boat.* I wanted to run, to shrink, to hide – somewhere, *anywhere* but we were on a boat and, even though it wasn't exactly dinghy-sized, I knew there was no escape and it would only be a matter of time before he saw me. I felt physically sick. Soon I would be shamelessly exposed as the fraud I was.

The sun was setting now and I managed to extricate myself away from Ellie who, slightly giddy from the bubbly, kept putting her arms around me and saying, 'I'm so proud of you jumping in like that; I mean I'd never have done it ...'

I moved through the crowd. It was cooler now that the sun was going down; soon darkness would be upon us and

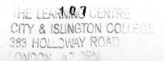

I felt a little relieved by this. I could hide better in the dark.

* * *

It was coming up for ten o'clock and the boat was in full swing. Despite the chill of the night air, many people were still in their bikinis or shorts, warmed by the day's earlier rays and hours of dancing. I, on the other hand, had brought a little denim mini to put on over my bikini and a soft knitted cream cardigan. I had also convinced Charlotte to lend me her Stetson in the hope that it might provide me with a disguise, enabling me to hide my face. I wrapped my cardigan round my shoulders and surveyed the scene from underneath Charlotte's hat. I decided to brave the semi-naked dancing bodies everywhere and make my way up to the top deck to go and watch the stars – I needed cheering up. I had a quick scan around to make sure Rex wasn't up there first though and when I saw that the coast was clear, my body, which had been rigid and stiff with panic since I'd seen him, began to loosen, just a little.

The top deck was less packed with people and there were groups of girls and guys sitting on the floor or on blankets that presumably they'd brought with them.

I stealthily slipped through the bodies, tilting my hat down over my face as far as it would go, and found a quiet corner where I could stand and look down at the sea from over the edge of the boat.

The moonlight hit the dark black water, illuminating the reflection of the boat's lights. Tiny beams shimmered and danced like naughty fairies across the surface, and I stood mesmerised for a few moments and leaned forward, resting my arms on the bars of the boat's edge, and let my chin sink on to my hands. *I should be sharing this moment with Rex,* I thought sadly. Here we both were, on the same boat at this amazing party, together but not together. He was so close that I could almost feel his presence, and it was torture not being able to lean back into his arms as he crossed them over my body and pulled me closer against his tanned and strong bare chest.

Instead, I was incognito underneath Charlotte's Stetson, slinking around in the shadows so as not to be seen like some kind of freaky cat-burglar.

I took a last look at the sea, its vast great blackness staring back at me, and turned to go.

'Oh God, Iz . . . IZ – Izzy, is that you?' Rex was standing in front of me, stooping down to get a better look underneath my hat. 'Oh my God, it is! Iz, what the hell are you doing here?' Before my brain could quite fully register his presence, he had picked me up and was twirling me around in the air and laughing and saying, 'You're here, you're here. This is mental!'

It felt so good to be held by him, even if I did feel a little light-headed after all that spinning. I was shaking uncontrollably, see-sawing between waves of extreme happiness and sharp shocks of blatant terror – he had found me. My quest to see the stars had brought him to me. I guess I should have known.

He was holding both my arms with his hands and beaming as he took a few steps back to look at me.

'I can't believe we've been on the same boat together

and haven't bumped into each other,' he said, his eyes shining wildly with what I hoped was happiness. 'How unlucky is that?' But luck had had little to do with it.

'I thought you were playing at Adam's Temple tonight,' I said, my eyes quickly darting around to check for an unexpected sister-arrival moment.

'Change of plan,' he said. 'Oh God, Iz, I'm gutted. You should have called. We could've hung out, really made a day of it and everything, especially since . . .' I knew he was about to say something like, 'especially since we haven't exactly got loads of time together'. But he stopped short of saying it and I wondered if it was to protect his own feelings as much as mine. *Does he really like me as much as I like him?*

'This is just amazing!' he said, picking me up again and spinning me round until I begged him to stop. 'Well, now that you're here, why don't you introduce me to these friends of yours? He smiled. 'Maybe I can introduce them to mine as well and we can all hang out.'

I had to think fast.

'Er, well, I would – if I could find them,' I said, laughing nervously. 'I've been looking for them for the last twenty minutes myself! I'm sure they'll turn up though, I mean it's not as if they could go very far, is it?'

Rex looked at me, beaming with surprise. He was wearing a thin cheesecloth shirt that was open, and the cut-off denim shorts I'd seen him in earlier, and he looked so gorgeous I wished that everyone else on the boat could just disappear and leave the two of us here alone together.

'Maybe they've been kidnapped by pirates,' he said,

laughing, 'made to walk the plank – *ooh arrrgggh*.' I forgot myself (and the situation) for a moment and started to giggle.

'Well, if we can't find your pals, then let's check mine out. Come on, we're all chillin' over here,' Rex said, leading me by the hand. I had no choice but to let him.

'Hey, Izzy,' Steve said, looking up. He seemed as surprised to see me as Rex had been. 'Have you been here all day?' He leaned in towards me and kissed both my cheeks, which shocked me a little. I wasn't used to people greeting me like this. It wasn't exactly something that the lads I knew back home did.

'Yeah,' I said, unable to stop thinking about Ellie – she would probably be wondering where the hell I was.

'I thought you . . . well, Rex said he was going to DJ at Adam's Temple, you see . . .'

'Last-minute change of plan.' He smiled. 'What a fantastic day though, eh? We've had a completely mental one, haven't we, Rex? Shame we never knew you were here. Who did you come with?'

They were all sitting down on a blanket on the floor of the top deck: Steve, a couple of other guys I'd never seen before and the two blondes from the other night, Chloe and Clare. They smiled at me enthusiastically. 'Hi honey!' Clare said. 'Not wearing your dancing shoes tonight then?'

'Thought it best to wear flip-flops,' I replied, the word 'flip-flops' sounding decidedly stupid as it left my lips.

'You know it, babes,' she said and I saw her turn to Chloe and say something but I couldn't make out what.

'I've lost my friends,' I said, trying not to sound like a child whose lost its mum in a shopping centre. 'But they're around somewhere . . . Erm, wasn't the DJing fantastic today?' I said, hoping that a change of subject would prevent any further questioning.

Rex nudged me softly in the ribs. 'Oh yeah?' he said, pretending to act hurt, 'not as good as mine I hope.'

'As if,' I replied, lowering my eyes a little and suddenly feeling shy.

'Well, you just chill out with us here, girl,' Steve said, patting the space next to him. 'This little spot is where it's all happening, dude.'

I smiled and looked at Rex, and he winked at me as we sat down.

'We're all heading off back to ours when the boat gets back,' he said. 'You've got to be there, Iz, bring your mates as well. It's not going to be too rowdy. Just some drinks and tunes and stuff.'

'What time does the boat get back again?' I enquired.

'Around midnight,' Steve said. 'That's when the real fun starts!'

'Worried you might turn into a pumpkin?' a female voice suddenly said from behind me. It was Jo-Jo. Queen of the one-liners, no less. She sat down gracefully next to Rex and looked at me, amused, waiting for a response.

'Jo,' Rex said sternly, giving her a warning look.

'Well, I – er, if I can find my friends, I'll ask them if they want to come,' I said, ignoring Jo-Jo's question and answering Rex's. I was visibly shaking now and Rex, having clearly noticed this, edged closer to me and put a reassuring arm around my waist – which while welcome, only seemed to make matters worse, and I shook more than ever.

'So tell me, Izzy,' began Jo-Jo, 'what *is* it that you do again?' She had reclined on to her side now, a position that I felt sure she knew accentuated her delicately slim curves, and was resting on her elbow.

'I'm at uni, studying to be a vet,' I said, quickly, trying to remember if I'd ever told her this in the first place and wondering why she was asking.

'A vet?' she said, pulling a face. 'You mean animals and stuff, right?'

'Yeah, animals and stuff,' I said, my voice trailing off towards the end.

'Sounds hideous,' Jo-Jo said, lighting a cigarette, 'having to stick your hand up cows' bums and all that messy business. Hardly a glamorous vocation, is it?' She began to laugh.

'Shut up, Jo,' Steve said, waving the smoke away from his face in annoyance. 'Has it ever crossed your champagne-addled mind that some people think there's more to life than fashion?'

Jo-Jo glared at him and turned back to face me.

'So how old will you be when you graduate?' she asked, looking at Rex, then Steve and finally, at me again.

I was rooted to the spot. I knew I would have to answer such a direct question – I was cornered. *Call me, Willow. Please, dear God, phone me now and save me!* But despite my best telepathic efforts, my phone didn't ring.

'I'll be twenty-five,' I said finally.

'Uh-huh,' Jo-Jo said, boring holes into me with her eyes. 'Couldn't do all that university stuff myself, being skint for years. Much better to be out there earning money. Me – well, as a part-time model and fashion designer, I don't get out of bed for less than —'

'Twenty quid,' Steve interjected, sarcastically. Rex started to laugh.

'Get stuffed, Steve,' Jo-Jo shot back, venomously.

'Guys, guys . . . please,' Rex intervened. 'If you can't say anything nice to each other then don't say anything at all.'

I shifted uncomfortably on the blanket. I was worried Jo-Jo was fishing for information because she didn't believe me. I suppose I couldn't really blame her. I had thought it was pretty amazing myself that no one had rumbled me already, because even though I knew I did look a bit older than sixteen, especially with the assistance of make-up and Ellie and Co.'s wardrobe additions, I felt sure I didn't look twenty-two either.

I had to think of something, an excuse to get away. Ellie would be starting to stress now and it would only be a matter of time before the search party would commence.

'Can I get anyone a drink?' I said, starting to get up, but Rex held me back slightly.

'It's OK, Iz,' he said softly, 'I'll go. You stay here. Steve will look after you.' He nodded at Steve, who nodded back in assurance. 'Beers all round, is it?'

I would have to leave while he was gone. I was out of my depth and I was convinced Jo-Jo knew it. Besides, the last thing I needed was for Ellie to catch me drinking beer.

Rex kissed me lightly on the cheek as he got up to make his way to the bar, and I wanted to leap into his arms. I would be safe there, away from Jo-Jo's persistent questions. I knew there was no going back now. It was bad enough that I had lied so blatantly about my age to him, but to do it in front of all his friends was the point of no return. He would be a laughing stock if they ever found out.

As soon as Rex disappeared into the crowd I made my excuses.

'Just nipping to the Ladies,' I said, mainly to Steve. 'Be back in a bit.'

'OK, darlin',' Steve said, and I felt a bit weird that he'd called me darlin', as if he knew me really well.

I could feel Jo-Jo's eyes on my back as I turned away, making it difficult for me walk normally, and I had to seriously concentrate on putting one foot in front of the other.

I could only have got a few steps when I saw Ellie striding towards me.

'There you are!' she said loudly. 'We've all been looking for you – *again*. Where have you been?'

I tried to edge her forward so that the others wouldn't be able to get a proper look, or worse, hear her.

'Just chatting to some people. What's the big deal, Ellie?' I said, crossly, my emotions beginning to spill over.

I glanced back over my shoulder; Jo-Jo was watching me. She had a wry smile on her face as she blew cigarette smoke from her mouth in an over-accentuated manner and mouthed to me, 'Everything OK?' I quickly smiled back and nodded.

'Who's that?' Ellie snapped, spotting Jo-Jo.

'Oh, er, just this girl I met. She's dead nice,' I said, clocking up another lie for the list.

'Aren't you going to introduce me then?' Ellie said, her tone relaxing slightly.

For a second I wished I had drowned when I had dive-bombed into the sea earlier, then I wouldn't be here, in this unbearable mess.

But it was too late. Before I could answer Ellie, I saw Rex making his way back towards us. He was carrying beers in both hands and trying to wave. There was no alternative. I had to make a run for it.

'Need the loo,' I said quickly, beginning to half-run in the other direction, leaving Ellie standing there, mouth open in confusion.

'Izzy!' I heard him calling my name. 'Iz, your bee—'

But I was already halfway down the stairs.

Chapter 13

C aught up in the excitement of the past few days, I'd almost completely forgotten about Edie. That was until she came looking for me. We were all having breakfast at the café by the swimming pool the following morning when I saw her purposefully striding our way. Frantic she would come running over and say something about the time I had cancelled on her, I had stuffed the remains of my croissant in my mouth and gulped the dregs of my orange juice and made my way towards her before she could reach us.

'Hey, Edie,' I said with a breezy smile and she kind of half smiled back, which worried me a little as I figured she was more upset with me than I thought.

'Listen, I'm so sorry about the other day. I've been feeling pretty poorly – food poisoning or something. Anyway, I'm better now, so if you fancy it, I thought maybe we could hang out a bit today?'

She had a blank look on her face. I could tell she didn't believe me.

'Yeah, OK,' she said, her expression changing from grim to a grin. 'I'm going to the games room now.' And by that I presumed she meant to add, 'So you had better come with me.'

Ellie had questioned me a little about my rushed exit on

the boat the previous evening, but I had talked my way out of it with quite some aplomb. I'd told Ellie I had come over all sick again and for fear of maybe throwing up there and then on the top deck in front of everyone – which even Ellie had to admit would've been simply hideous – I had run off to chuck up in the loos. Ellie had eventually found me and taken me to the captain's quarters, where I was able to lie down (or rather, hide) for the duration of the trip. When we docked at the marina, I had rushed off the boat so fast that Ellie had struggled to keep up with me. As a result, she had sworn she would take me to a doctor first thing this morning, but I had assured her I now felt one hundred per cent better and ate two helpings of pancakes with maple syrup to prove it.

Explaining to Rex, on the other hand, was going to be another matter entirely. He had left me three messages from last night. The first sounded almost jovial: 'Hey Iz, where are you? You just zipped off. Your beer's getting warm. I'm still on the top deck waiting for you.' The second sounded more urgent: 'It's been over half an hour. I'm worried, Iz. I can't find you. Are you OK? Did I do something? *Please* call me.' His third and final message had a different, more sombre tone and it had made me feel sick when I heard it: 'Iz, it's me. I've searched the boat and I can't find you anywhere. I guess you must still be here – if you want to be found, let me know. But you know, if you don't, well, that's fair enough.' He had sounded upset, even a little angry. Who could blame him? I had disappeared without trace, leaving him standing there looking like a chump in front of his friends, wondering what the hell had happened.

'We're off to the games room for a bit,' I said to Ellie.

'OK, babes, we'll be round here until late if you need us,' Ellie said, gesturing towards the sun loungers by the pool that might as well have been emblazoned with their names, given the amount of time they had spent on them.

So Edie was on one side of the Daytona machine and I was on the other. We were racing against each other and she was thrashing me. *Driver One Wins* flashed over our screens and she gave a little 'whoo-hoo' as she punched the air in victory.

'So,' Edie said, as she began inserting coins into another of the games machines, 'that time you cancelled when we were supposed to go to the beach, it didn't have anything to do with a guy, did it?'

I was dumbfounded. How had she guessed? I mean, there I was, lying my face off to my sister who had known me all my life and who was that much older and supposedly wiser, and here was Edie, this goofy fourteen-year-old who I'd only met a couple of times in my life, who had sussed me out completely.

'How did you know that?' I asked, trying to keep my cool and not give too much away.

'You're a terrible liar,' she said, although not maliciously. 'So is that why you looked like you were going to choke on your croissant when you saw me coming over, because you thought I might say something to your sister? Doesn't she know about him or something?'

I was beginning to wonder if Edie was psychic.

'Listen, Edie,' I said, moving my chair closer in to hers in a conspiratorial way, 'I've met this amazing man and I can't tell my sister about him because, well, it's complicated, so you know, I kind of need a good alibi and I was hoping . . .'

I had nothing to lose by asking her outright if she'd cover for me. She'd pretty much guessed my game anyway and I figured it would be best to have her on side rather than lie to her, because all this lying business was becoming massively stressful and complex.

'Well, the thing is, I would, no problems, but we're going home tomorrow,' Edie said, looking a little crestfallen.

'Oh,' I said, matching her expression. I was gutted, because all the time I could say I was with Edie I knew Ellie wouldn't worry. Edie was here with her parents, so Ellie knew that wherever Edie was, they weren't too far behind and therefore I was safe.

I felt a bit sad too, because now I knew she was going home, I wished I had managed to spend more time with Edie. I sensed I would like Edie more once I got to know her better and that she was probably a lot of fun, as well as intuitive. I vowed to try and squeeze in an afternoon at the beach with her by way of saying goodbye.

'But you know, you could always *still* say you were with me . . . You're desperate to see this lad, right?' she said, seemingly enjoying the whole subterfuge of the conversation. 'So, it's simple: don't tell your sister we've gone home. Just pretend I'm still here and everything's normal and that you're still hanging out with me!'

I stared back at the face opposite me and felt like grabbing it and planting a kiss on each plump, pink cheek.

'Edie – Edie . . . ?' and I realised I didn't know her last name.

'Price,' she said helpfully.

'Edie Price,' I announced, '*you* are an absolute genius!'

'Thanks!' she said, smiling wickedly. 'I reckon that's worth holding on to that Dude Sound CD, don't you?' And I had to admit that it was.

Chapter 14

I t had taken all the courage I had to call Rex when I went back up to the apartment. I was terrified he would be upset, or worse, angry with me for running off. I had to try and explain, to make it up to him and apologise.

The conversation had started off uncomfortably. 'Well, hello stranger,' he said, in measured tones. 'What happened to *you* last night?'

'Oh Rex, I'm so sorry,' I said, panic rising in my throat. 'I was taken ill suddenly – must've been food poisoning or something. I had to rush off because I thought I was going to be si— well, you know, ill.' I didn't much relish the distinctly unattractive idea of Rex imagining me bent double over a toilet bowl, throwing my guts up, but I preferred it to the truth. 'I'm so, so sorry to have just left you there like that – will you forgive me?'

There was a pause before he said quietly, 'You should have called me. I was so worried. I spent the rest of the night searching for you. I thought I'd done something to upset you. Why didn't you call?'

I braced myself. I had rehearsed this lie over in my mind before phoning him, but still I was scared I would stuff it up and trip over my words.

'I couldn't call. I was so sick that I had to go and lie down in the captain's quarters until we docked. I could hardly speak for being ill and my friends were so worried they thought they might have to take me to a hospital.' I winced as I said it, horrified at my own ability to tell such blatant lies.

There was another pause and I held my breath, waiting for his response.

'Well, I'm just glad you're OK. You *are* OK, aren't you?' he asked, concerned.

'Yes, much better, thanks. I'm sorry,' I said again. I felt terrible.

'Stop saying you're sorry,' he said, softly. 'It couldn't be helped.'

'I'm sorry. I'll stop saying I'm sorry,' I replied, and we both laughed a little shakily.

'Forgive me if my last message sounded harsh,' he said. 'I had no idea you were ill. I just thought you'd gone and left me and, well, all sorts of horrible stuff went through my mind. I wracked my brain trying to remember if I'd said or done something that would make you run off like that, but I couldn't think . . .'

He sounded so insecure, and I wished I was standing in front of him so I could hold him and reassure him.

'You've got nothing to be sorry about,' I said. 'You weren't to know.'

'Maybe it was the lobster,' he said.

'The lobster?'

'That made you ill. You've got to be careful with seafood, you know – botulism.'

'Maybe I'm just lovesick,' I said quietly, not sure whether I should push it because he might still be a little annoyed with me, even if he didn't sound it now.

'Nah, can't have been that,' he said.

'Why not?' I asked.

'Because then I'd have got ill as well,' he said.

I felt a wave of relief and happiness. When he said things like that, I felt sure that he loved me as well. And it felt so good I wanted to bathe in the warm glow of his words, let them surround me and caress me and fill me with hope and confidence.

'If you're feeling up to it, perhaps you'd like to come to the market with me later?' he asked tentatively. 'Or, I could always come to you and nurse you better . . .'

'The market sounds perfect,' I said, quickly. 'I'd love to come.'

I put the phone down and smiled. It was going to be OK. I was forgiven.

The hippy market at Es Cana was buzzing with shoppers that afternoon. Enticing smells of freshly-cooked food wafted out from various stalls and the place was awash with colour. Rex took my hand as we strolled past the many people selling exotic batik clothing and handmade leather goods, and I breathed in the thick smell of joss sticks in the air.

'Only ten euro!' a trader shouted, holding up a pink leather handbag that had a long strap on it. 'Look good, look good,' he called to me as we walked past.

Rex waved his hand, '*Non, gracias,*' he smiled at him kindly. 'Hey, Iz, I want to show you something,' he said, pulling me over towards this little stall that was full of beads and bright trinkets, A very old, skinny, dark-skinned man, sat by it, his face all leathery-looking and wrinkled from the sun. '*Hola Juan Pablo, me allegro de volver a verle,*' said Rex, holding out his hands, and I gathered that this must be the hippy guy he had told me about. They embraced warmly, and the old man said something in Spanish to Rex and Rex laughed a little and pulled me closer to him, proudly.

'*Si, si . . . una chica muy guapa!*' Rex beamed, and I was desperate to know what this meant, but didn't like to ask. Either way, it had sounded like Juan Pablo had paid me a compliment so I wasn't too worried.

'Choose something you like,' Rex said, gesturing to the piles of silver jewellery displayed on the table.

'No, I couldn't!' I replied, embarrassed.

'Don't be daft. Please, I want to buy you something, anything – just choose something you like.'

'No, really.'

The old hippy guy looked at us, amused by our squabbling. But Rex was insistent, so he picked out this amazing little bracelet with tiny silver bells on it and it was just so beautiful and unusual that I fell in love with it instantly, just like I did for him.

The sun was beating down on us and we decided to take shelter in a small outdoor café that had huge red-and-white striped umbrellas, and Rex ordered us two strawberry lassis.

'I love my present,' I said, turning my wrist to the side

slightly to inspect my new gift. 'It's really beautiful.'

'The bells make a little jingly sound whenever you move. That means I'll be able to tell when you're sneaking up on me,' he laughed.

'Sneaking up on people is *your* job!' I protested, thinking of all the times he'd popped up from behind me this holiday. 'Thanks for bringing me here today,' I said, being serious for a moment, 'for being my own private tour guide.'

'It's been my pleasure.' He smiled. 'But there are so many other places I want to take you to. There's so much I'd love you to see. The mountains, for one thing – they're absolutely breathtaking. And then there's Pepe's Bar – this tiny little restaurant just north of Es Cana. It serves the most amazing food: fresh paella and mussels and shrimps . . .'

'Ugh, don't bring up seafood,' I said, pulling a face and clutching my stomach, attempting to validate the whole food-poisoning lie from the boat party.

'Hey, *I* didn't bring it up – *you* did!' He gave me a careful look, checking to see if he'd overstepped the mark and caused offence.

'Oh ha, ha, very funny,' I said, smiling sarcastically.

I knew he was just trying to make light of it, make me laugh and see the funny side. I thought it was maybe his way of saying all was forgiven. 'A joker as well as every-thing else,' I scoffed. 'Is there no end to your list of talents?'

'Now let me see . . .' Rex said, putting a finger up to his mouth in an overstated pondering gesture. He was pretending to count on his fingers and was muttering under his breath. 'Superstar DJ . . . yes . . . er, stunning guitar player and musician, world-class diver and fisherman – check . . . great cook and —'

I picked up a beer mat from the table and threw it at him. He put his hand up to his face and laughed.

'Seriously though, I want to take you everywhere with me. Show you *everything*,' he said. 'There's so much I want you to see and do and so little . . .'

I knew he was about to say 'time' and I was glad when he didn't finish the sentence.

Bringing up the subject of me leaving to go home would have spoiled the perfectly lovely and flirty banter we were enjoying.

I was touched that he wanted to take me everywhere with him. I wanted him to show me all the places he'd been to and loved. I knew that with each outing I would discover a little bit more about him – the story of his life. And I wanted to be part of that story more than anything in the world.

Right then, I vowed that I would tell him the truth soon, because I hated the fact that I was keeping something from him. You just don't keep secrets from the people you love, do you?

'You're so different from how I thought you would be when I first met you,' I found myself saying. 'I thought you'd be . . .' I paused.

'Go on . . . tell me . . . what did you think? I'd really like to know,' he said, cocking his head to one side.

'Well, I guess that, being a DJ, I just thought you'd be

this really flashy type. But you're not like that at all – you're kind and thoughtful and you care about people and you love animals —'

'And butterflies,' he added.

'And butterflies . . . and you have all these strong principles. You've got time for people who aren't like you or who fit into a "cool" gang. And you're sensitive and you like love songs . . . You're just wonderful, I suppose.'

Rex was smiling at me now, a huge cat-that-got-the-cream smile, and I playfully pushed him. 'Yes, I am wonderful, aren't I?'

'Oh and add "modest" to that list too!' I laughed, pushing him again. 'And what about me?' I asked, because I really wanted to know how he felt about me too. 'What did you think of me when we first met?'

Usually, I'd never have been brave enough to ask anyone such a question. But I was so at ease with Rex that it felt natural.

'You? Well, I thought you were OK I suppose,' he said teasing me.

'No, seriously,' I said, shifting with anticipation in my seat.

'Well in that case,' he said, taking me by the hand, 'when I first saw you at Alfredo's, I just knew I had to get to know you.' Absentmindedly playing with my fingers, he continued, 'There was something in your eyes when I stopped you that time and directed you to the toilet . . .'

I blushed as I remembered how I had felt: awkward and embarrassed, yet delighted.

'Something infinitely kind. It was endearing, the way you looked so uncomfortable. I felt drawn to you. That's why I followed you outside. You had this aura about you. I know it sounds like a line, and a cheesy one, but I felt sure there was this spiritual connection between us. Call it chemistry, magic, whatever, but it was so strong. And of course, there's the fact that you're very beautiful,' he said, as if it were the most obvious thing in the world. 'I couldn't take my eyes off you. You stood out from the crowd. And now that I know you, now that we've managed to spend some time together, I realise I was right. You have a heart the size of Manchester and your smile lights up a room. Like I said before, I feel I've known you for ever. I *hope* I know you for ever.'

I was stunned into silence. I looked at him, paralysed in my chair, unable to speak, to take in his words. No one had ever said anything like this to me in my life before. How had he seen so much in me, whereas others before him had seen nothing? Up until now, no one had ever looked past my awkwardness. In the eyes of most lads I knew, I felt sure I just blended into the background. I was Willow Roberts's mate, the one with the mad hair that didn't say much. No one had ever bothered to try and discover who I really was and the things I thought and felt. But it didn't matter whether I believed I was all those things myself. If Rex thought so, that was all that mattered.

Chapter 15

I t was Sunday and I was back at the apartment doodling on a piece of paper and thinking about the past week's events.

I picked my phone up to text Willow. I wondered why she hadn't been texting me every day like she had promised. Could it be that she was too busy hanging out with her new best friend to bother? Would it look like I was desperate if I kept on texting her first? The thought made me miserable. Things had always been so spontaneous between us, but now everything felt different – like I needed to consider what I would say.

In the absence of knowing what else to write, I sent her a little smiley face icon that winked and underneath I wrote, WISH YOU WERE HERE, IZ X

It wasn't a lie either. I really did wish she was here. I felt sure, in my heart of hearts, that if Willow had been here in Ibiza, I wouldn't need to worry about anything much at all, least of all Ellie and the lies I had been telling her. Willow would've made the perfect alibi and I knew that she would've had Ellie wrapped round her little finger, just like she does with everyone else.

Despite a few near misses and all the stress and trauma these had brought with them, lying to Ellie had been, in the grand scheme of things, much easier than I had bargained on, particularly since Edie's genius little plan seemed to be working a treat. As a result, the past few days I'd been managing to slip away to see Rex and we'd been spending afternoons on the beach, our beach, messing about in the sea and sunning our bodies next to each other or zipping down to Ibiza Town on his moped to window-shop in all the posh boutiques. Sometimes though, Rex had things to do; gigs to arrange, club owners to liaise with and he spent time practising his sets with Steve.

I understood. After all, he'd had a life before he met me and couldn't just drop everything to kick back with me on the beach all day, even if he had wanted to – which he'd assured me he did. Although knowing this brought me some comfort, I had to keep reminding myself that I was on holiday and that Ibiza was his life and that included work and all the day-to-day drudgery, even if it was set against such a beautiful, scenic backdrop. 'Still got to work, even if the sun's shining,' he'd said to me one day when he couldn't meet me. But it was little consolation.

I missed him like crazy when we were apart although I tried my best not to make him feel bad about it; even if I felt sure the disappointment at not being able to spend all our time together was written on my face. To try and redress the balance a bit, I had decided that I would go to the beach with Edie before she went home, like I had promised. So on the Tuesday, while Rex was zipping around the island with Steve arranging that night's DJ set and generally being a man about town, I sloped off to Playa d'en Bossa with her for a couple of hours before her flight in the evening and, presumably as a parting gift, her parents let her go with me alone.

'So do you reckon this lad is in love with you then?' Edie had asked me as she bobbed up and down in the sea on her embarrassing crocodile lilo (note: I'd borrowed Charlotte's pink lilo, which was much less conspicuous).

'Oh, I really don't know,' I'd said, my eyes closed as I let my arms and legs flop into the cool water beneath me. I had felt a little embarrassed talking about it.

'I reckon he is,' she'd said, smugly.

I opened my eyes this time and squinted in the sunlight to get a better look at her expression.

'What makes you say that?' I'd asked, intrigued.

'Oh I don't know.' Edie had shrugged dramatically. 'You have the air of a woman who is loved about you.'

I'd laughed because it seemed such a funny thing for anyone to say, not least a fourteen-year-old, but I also felt quite chuffed because, looking back, Edie had been pretty spot on about Rex and me so far and I hoped she was right.

'Will you write to me when you get back to England?' she had asked, hope apparent in her tone. 'I'll give you my e-mail address.'

'Of course,' I promised, and this time I really meant it.

That same afternoon, after I'd said goodbye to Edie and Rex had finished his chores, he took me to lunch at Pepe's Bar, like he'd promised to, and we sampled some of that infamous paella he'd raved about.

On the way there, we'd spotted something lying in the

road. Rex had pulled over so we could take a look, and when we got closer we realised it was a bird. It had probably been hit by a passing car or bike and was in its final death throes; its once strong and colourful wings flapping pathetically as it yelped and squawked. 'We've got to do something,' I pleaded, crouching down and trying to pick up the distressed creature. 'It'll die if we don't do something . . .'

But, sensing danger, the bird became even more frantic and made this horrible, screaming sound, desperate to escape.

'It's OK,' Rex said gently, a reassuring tone in his voice. 'I know what to do.' He knelt down next to me and I looked at him, desolate. Slowly and carefully, he held his hands out towards the bird and started making a funny cooing noise. '*Cooooo, coooooo* . . . There, there,' he said. 'It's OK, little fella. We won't hurt you . . .' Eventually the little bird was perfectly still, its dark black eyes blinking back at Rex as he tenderly picked it up in his hands and gently placed it down underneath a small tree.

I stood transfixed by the way the bird had just let him pick it up without a fuss.

'How did you do that?'

'The cooing noise,' Rex said, pulling some leaves and a bit of greenery in around the bird to protect it. 'They recognise it. It's a bit like talking to them.'

'Do you think it will die?' I asked thinly, looking down at the tiny, helpless little bird and suddenly feeling a profound sadness.

Rex stood up and turned to look at me. He held out his

hand for me to take it and pulled me close. It was warm in his arms and I could feel the softness of the skin on his neck against my cheek.

'Oh, Iz,' he said. I knew he was thinking the same thing as me; I could see the same sadness in his eyes as my own. I had thought of my dad when I saw that poor wretched creature lying helpless in the road and I felt sure he had thought of this too. That's why he had done his best to try and save it.

'Thank you,' I whispered. He didn't need to ask me why I was thanking him. At that moment our hearts and minds were in sync with each other, and I was sure he already knew.

The moment with the bird had touched me so deeply. Seeing the kindness in him, how gentle and sensitive he could be, had made me fall in love with him just that little bit more, if that was at all possible.

I had held on to this feeling in the week that followed, as we drank coffee by the marina and watched the boats that were moored there bobbing up and down in the water. We talked about what we would name our yacht if – or as Rex had said, *when* we owned one ourselves, and whenever he said things like that, little things that suggested there was a future for us and that there would still be a 'we' even after I'd gone home, my heart would leap up into my throat and my stomach would twist in knots. By now, the thought of me leaving him was indescribable and when my mind tricked itself into thinking about it, just for a split second, it felt like someone was reaching deep inside me, pulling my heart out through my mouth. I couldn't even begin to imagine how I was going to feel when the time came for me to say goodbye. So I did what I always do. I pretended it wasn't going to happen, even though, of all people, I should really have known better.

The sound of my phone beeping snapped me back to reality. I stopped doodling and went to my bag to retrieve it. Rex had left me a message. I hadn't even heard it ring and felt anxious that I had missed his call.

'Hey gorgeous . . .' There was a slight pause. 'Er – not sure if this is recording . . . It's me by the way, Rex. You know that *crazy* DJ bloke who's *crazy* about you. Listen, two things. First up, I *have* to see you tonight. No excuses . . . There was another pause. 'Anyway – er, the second thing is, I've got an idea for the name of that boat we're going to have some day. Remember when we were down by the marina looking at them the other night? Well, how about *Ritmo de la Noche*? It means "rhythm of the night". I thought it sounded quite cool, you know, with the whole DJ connection and everything . . . Well, anyway, I'm waffling now – and erm, your phone is saying something to me. Please try and —'

'End of message!' the recorded voice said abruptly, and I clutched the phone to my chest and shut my eyes. I made a mental note never to delete the message, so that whenever we were apart I'd feel close to him and could hear him telling me over and over again that he was crazy about me.

I called him back.

'Listen, can you meet me?' he asked.

'I can try,' I said, mentally planning my escape from Ellie and Co.

'Please try. There's something I want you to see.'

'Really? What?'

'You'll find out,' he said, sounding pleased with himself.

'OK, well, you say goodbye first then,' I said.

'Goodbye first,' he said.

'Goodbye second,' I said, and reluctantly I clicked off my phone.

I knew I had to meet him, find out what it was that he so desperately wanted to show me. I told Ellie I was going out with Edie and her parents to some Spanish dancing evening at a restaurant and would probably be back a bit late. It was shocking how easily the ever-more creative lies were beginning to fall from my lips. Ellie seemed none the wiser though and if she had guessed anything was up, she sure as hell wasn't letting on about it. She was probably secretly pleased I was spending all this time with Edie, bogus though it was, because it meant she could go off clubbing with her mates. This way, she didn't need to ask too many questions.

I managed to sneak off before the others came back from the pool to do their ritual getting-ready-to-go-out session and ran down to the lilo shop to meet him.

As soon as he saw me he got off his bike and held me in his arms for ages, only momentarily breaking off to kiss me.

'I'm so glad you came,' he said softly. 'I don't know why, but I suddenly had this feeling that you might cancel.'

I shook my head. 'Don't be daft,' I said. 'The world would have to stop turning before I would cancel on you.'

He stood there frozen in this funny pose and I realised he was making out that the world had really stopped and he'd been frozen in time.

I laughed and he seemed glad that he'd made me smile. 'Why would you think I'd cancel?' I asked.

'Oh, I don't know,' Rex said, avoiding my gaze. 'These friends of yours . . . I thought maybe they'd start getting fed up with the fact that we're spending so much time together. I mean, you are supposed to be on holiday with them after all.'

'Don't worry about them,' I said. 'They're happy for me.'

I felt a bit sick as I said it and I wondered if they really would be happy for me if they knew the truth.

The sun was setting as we pulled up at the side of the dusty road. We were high up on a mountain and even though I had no real idea of where we were it all seemed strangely familiar, the fragrant scent of the pine trees in the air and lush green hills sheltering us.

'Come on,' he said, and he held my hand as we walked a little way up the mountainside. We reached a little clearing at the edge of the mountain and I looked out towards the sea. The sunset was as beautiful as ever, if not more so tonight, the rich golds mixing with the deep red and splashes of purple, and I could tell it was going to be another beautiful day tomorrow. I squeezed his hand tightly.

'Look down,' he said, and he pulled me a little closer to

the edge of the mountain so I could get a better view. And then I saw it.

In the bay below us, written in the sand with pebbles and shells were the words, *I LOVE YOU ISABELLE* surrounded by a giant heart also made from pebbles and stones that he'd obviously hand-picked from the shore. It looked so huge from up here it made me wonder just how big it really was down there, and I figured that it must've taken him ages – maybe even the whole day – to collect all those stones and turn them into something so beautiful. I gasped as I turned to look at him, standing there in front of me, his green eyes shining brightly and smiling his perfect smile.

I was smiling too, only I realised that tears were falling from my face as well. I was so blown away by it. I was so happy that he felt the same: he loved me. *Oh God, he really loved me!* Yet through my happiness was this infinite sadness too. I had not told the truth about myself and therefore I couldn't allow myself to fully believe it was all real. I wondered if the two, happiness and sadness, were forever intertwined, one not existing without the other. Just like me and him.

I turned to face him, the last of the fading sun's rays casting light on to his hair. We held each other and kissed deeply, with a sense of urgency that, it seemed, until now we had only just touched upon, and I wanted to drown in his deep, sea-green eyes. We both knew time was running out for us. I would be going home in a week. Yet I knew deep in my heart, unlike the sun that was fading behind us, the love I felt for him never would.

Chapter 16

It was getting late and we decided to stop off at Rex's place in Es Cana to sample those olives he had told me about. It was the most perfect little whitewashed house ever, with a shock of pink flowers growing up the side. Rex told me that the flowers were called bougainvillea and had picked some for me to put in my hair, which I gladly did because anything that made my hair look nicer was all right in my book.

I was slightly apprehensive about going back to Rex's house. Having already shown me most of his regular haunts and places of personal meaning, it seemed as though this was the last place he wanted me to see – like in showing me, he was revealing the final aspect of himself.

It was a warm, balmy evening and Rex suggested we sit in the garden that was full of flowers and little trees and plants and shrubs, their scent filling the air with a pungent aroma. Underneath a tree was one of those swinging benches with a canopy over the top. I almost squealed with delight when I saw it. My sister and I had always wanted one as kids.

We both fell backwards on to the bench and began to swing, the soft evening breeze and heady smell of the flowers wafting past our noses as we rocked.

'It's beautiful here,' I said as I tentatively placed the

olive that he'd given me in my mouth – and it actually tasted OK, nothing like the ones Willow and I had sampled back home. 'I can see why you'd never want to come home.'

'This *is* my home,' Rex said, letting one leg dangle over the edge of the bench as it swung. 'I will never leave here. Ibiza is where my heart is. I've never felt more at home anywhere in the world – and you know, I've travelled a bit: all over Europe, Thailand, Bali, across Asia, Australia, New Zealand, America, Mexico and of course, Manchester.' He laughed.

I was pretty impressed. This was only my third time abroad, unless you count a day trip to Calais with the school when I was twelve, in which case it was my fourth.

'Although my family are back in England, I don't think of it as home,' he said. 'You know when you're away in a different place and you dream of home? Well, Ibiza is where I dream of, even though I've only been here for five years.'

All this talk of home made me think about my own: my home in London with Mum and Ellie and Greg. I thought of my bedroom – my small, cosy bedroom with the pale-pink walls that badly needed redecorating, and my fairy lights in the shape of hearts around my bed, with my big warm duvet and fluffy pillows, and my books and CDs and my clothes and shoes and bags strewn across the floor. I suddenly missed it, missed my mum and, shocked as I was to admit it, even Greg too. Abruptly I craved the uncomplicated normality of it all, the predictability of my pre-Ibiza life and the hustle and bustle of my daily routine:

going to school, hanging out with Wils, doing nothing much in particular. Everything had seemed so straightforward before I'd come here. It had been simple and familiar, which made me feel safe. I wondered if, on my return, everything would just slot right back into its old place, or would things have irrevocably changed, especially now that Wils had found a new friend and I had fallen in love?

'But, you see, a house isn't a home unless there's love there . . .' Rex said, breaking my thoughts.

'No, I guess not,' I said with a smile and I thought about how much love there was and had been in my house over the years. 'No one's ever done anything like that for me before – you know, the letters in the sand,' I said, referring to his pledge on the beach. 'It was so . . . so lovely.'

'I meant it, you know,' he said, shuffling in closer to me. 'I wanted to do something special for you.'

I sensed he was thinking about the whole time-running-out issue again but I couldn't bring it up. It hurt too much to even think about it, let alone say it out loud.

'It *was* special,' I said, and he would never really know how much.

'*You're* special,' he said, looking at me, his eyes filled with sincerity. 'You know, I'll be twenty-seven soon and although it's not exactly old, I was beginning to wonder if I'd ever find you . . .'

I looked up at him now, entranced by what he was saying.

'I know I live in this crazy, hedonistic world filled with parties and eternal sunshine, but one day I knew I'd meet someone that would change the way I feel about my future, someone I could envisage spending my life with: marriage and a family – all that is really important to me. I'm actually quite traditional at heart,' he said, seeming a little shy all of a sudden.

I swallowed dryly, unsure of how to feel. His words both scared and exhilarated me simultaneously. Was he saying it was me? *I* was the one he wanted to grow old with?

'When I was twenty-two, your age, I was bang on it,' he continued. 'Music and partying was all I ever thought about. I never thought about tomorrow, let alone the next ten years. But you know since meeting you, I've thought more about my future and what I want from it than ever before.'

I looked down at my feet, uncertain of how to respond. I wished I could fast-forward my life ten years – to be twenty-six, the same age as him. I wanted to want those things too: marriage, children, a home life with a man I loved. I wanted to have them with him – but right now hearing him talk about them made them seem so real and it felt strange. Rex was still looking at me intensely and I smiled at him nervously.

'Don't worry,' he said, sensing my discomfort. 'I'm not about to whisk you down the aisle or anything. Not just yet anyway,' he laughed and took my hand. 'When do you have to go?' he asked, squeezing it tightly.

'Well, I said I would probably be back before it got too late.'

'No, I mean go *home*, back to London?' His voice was wavering. He'd finally been the braver of us both and had brought up the subject of me leaving.

'Next Monday,' I said quietly. And we both sat there, the sadness of those inevitable words hanging there, mixed with the scent of the flowers in the air.

'Well,' he said, finally, 'in that case I don't want to waste a second.' He began rocking the bench really high, back and forth, and I began to shriek because I thought the whole thing might collapse any second.

'Enough!' I screamed and I tried to stop him, but he grabbed me by the waist and started tickling me, and I was gasping for breath – and sure enough, the rope that was supporting the battered old swing bench finally gave way under the strain and we crashed down on the grass with a bump.

We both sat there, looking at each other a bit bewildered, before we cracked up laughing, rolling around on the grass, our faces aching as we collapsed in a hysterical heap next to each other and we were looking up at the sky that was close to darkness by now.

'You know I love you too,' I found myself saying, after a moment's silence.

Rex touched my hand softly, linking his fingers through mine, creating a lock as he pulled me over on top of him so that our bodies were touching. I snuggled against his chest, listening to the sound of his heart as he spoke.

'It's funny,' he said, 'falling in love was the last thing I had expected. There I am playing my music and strumming my guitar, and then suddenly you come along and it all feels so different. Now when I pick up my guitar I think of songs I'd like to play for you. Whenever I spin a record, it reminds me of things we've done or a place we've been to together. Everything I say and do, all that I see and hear, relates back to you – to us – and it just feels so right. And now – well, you'll be going home soon and I just . . . well, that just seems so wrong.'

I felt so sad – sad because I felt all those things and more. With Rex I felt truly alive, like I had been dead all these years and he had woken me from an eternal sleep, and soon it would all be gone.

'You know I really do love you too,' I repeated, because now that I'd found the courage to say it once I wanted to keep on saying it and saying it until I wore the words out.

Rex pulled me even closer to him, as if he wanted to pull me right into his soul, and he stroked my hair, over and over.

'That time,' he said as his gentle fingers worked their way through my knotty mass of curls, 'on the beach when you told me about your dad. I knew then that I loved you.'

'You did?' I asked, willing him to continue.

'You opened up to me and it made me feel special, like you trusted me enough with your deepest feelings. I felt honoured that you could share your pain with me and it made me want to never let anything or anyone hurt you ever again.'

I could feel tears forming in my eyes, making the image of his face all blurry as I looked at him.

'I thought about what you'd told me when I went for my daily run along the beach the next day and you know, I cried, Iz. I cried for that little eleven-year-old girl you were who had lost her dad in such a cruel way. I felt your pain as if it were my own. That's when I knew I must love you.'

I let the tears silently slide down the side of my face again and he bent forward and kissed me. His lips were soft and warm and his breath was bittersweet, mixed with the saltiness of my tears. 'I never want to let you go,' he said, his voice cracking as he held on to me.

'Then don't,' I croaked back. 'Don't ever let me go.'

When I woke, the sun was shining brightly, and I shut my eyes as quickly as I had opened them to shield them from its harshness. For a second I didn't know where I was and I felt a brief moment of panic. Then I felt Rex's arm around me, loosely draped over my shoulder as he lay next to me on the sofa. I wasn't sure how we had got there, or what time it was, or whether I should wake him – he looked so peaceful asleep next to me, the softness of his breathing only just audible. We must've fallen asleep on his couch.

I searched for my phone to check the time. Oh bloody hell! It was nearly eight o'clock in the morning – the *next* morning. And now the panic really did set in. I was for the high jump now, of that much I was sure.

Chapter 17

The second I walked through the door and clocked Ellie's face, I was hit by this sinking feeling, the sort I imagine criminals must have when they come home to find the police waiting for them, knowing they've been caught bang to rights.

'Been anywhere nice?' said Ellie, her voice tight and measured.

'Not really – well, yes actually, I had a really nice night with Edie. We went for pizza and then back to her apartment to listen to CDs and it got late and well, I thought I might as well stay over. Sorry I didn't text but I fell asleep . . .'

My sister stood up and walked towards me, and I couldn't help but notice how gracefully she moved, like a ballerina, which was a ridiculous thing to notice, given the circumstances.

'So are you going to tell me where you *really* were or are you just going to carry on with these blatant lies?' Ellie asked angrily. 'I know that Edie girl went home *over a week ago!*' she said, emphasising the final part for maximum impact.

I knew the time had come.

'OK,' I said, defeated, 'I'll tell you everything.' And so I did. Well, sort of.

I told her how I'd met someone that I really liked and

that we'd been spending some time together. I'd been worried that she would be worried if I told her about it and I wanted to keep it a secret because I didn't want everyone to know. I figured that it was just easier to lie than tell the truth. I missed out the part about Rex being a twenty-six-year-old DJ with his own moped, though, because I knew she'd totally freak – and I was in enough trouble already.

'Why didn't you just tell me you'd met someone?' Ellie asked when I had finished, her voice softening slightly. 'I wouldn't have minded you spending some time with a lad. Anyway who is he? I suppose you were with him last night?'

'Yes,' I said weakly.

'*All* night?'

I nodded. There was no point in lying any more. I was too tired.

'But we just fell asleep, *honestly*,' I added. 'I'm sorry. I know I should've just told you the truth from the start.'

Ellie looked at me mournfully and shook her head. 'I trusted you, Iz,' she said, 'brought you out here, with *my* friends on *my* holiday because you're always going on and on about how much you want to be included and be grown-up and ... and ... then you disappear for hours on end every day and I realise you've been lying to me about where you've been and who you've been with.'

'Are you going to tell Mum about this?' I asked, pathetically.

'I haven't decided yet,' she answered crisply. 'I was so worried. I'd tried to call you on your mobile a dozen times to see if you wanted to come with us to a beach barbecue, but it just kept going straight to voicemail. So I went down to reception and asked them what apartment that Edie girl and her family were in and I was so shocked when they told me that they had already flown back to England. I panicked and suddenly had all these horrible thoughts of you lying in a ditch somewhere; raped, murdered – anything!' Ellie was pacing the room, waving her arms manically. 'Why didn't you want me to know that you'd met someone? Is he a criminal? A drug-dealer or something?'

'No!' I said, choking back the sobs. 'He's amazing and kind and gentle and loving. He respects me and says he loves me and I believe him, but he's, well, a bit older than me and I didn't think you'd approve.'

'Older?' Ellie said, frowning, 'How much older?' Her voice was high-pitched and angry now and my head started to hurt.

'He's twenty-six,' I sighed, and it was a relief to have finally said it out loud, to tell the truth.

'Twenty-six?' she said, as she fell on to the bed in shock.

'And he's got a moped and he's a DJ,' I said quickly, because I thought if I said it fast enough she might not hear.

'A DJ? And I suppose you've been on his moped?'

'His name's Rex and yes, I have, a few times,' I said, remorsefully.

She seemed more composed now and I sensed that she knew I was finally telling the truth.

'Do you mean Rex 'The Dex', the DJ from Café Del Sol?' She looked at me, eyes wide with horror, but somewhere, blink and you'd have missed it, I was sure I saw a flash of something else – admiration perhaps?

'That's him,' I said, wishing he could just zip right up on his moped so I could ride off with him and not have to face any of this.

'Right! I know where to find him and when I do, I'm going to kill him,' she said in her scary calm voice again. 'You're only sixteen years old, for Christ's sake! I mean, what's he playing at? He's older than Tom! Is he some kind of cradle-snatcher or something?'

This was exactly the type of reaction I had feared most and I broke down in tears.

'He doesn't know I'm only sixteen,' I whispered, just loud enough for her to hear.

Ellie sat there on the bed, staring at me in disbelief.

'You didn't tell him you were only sixteen? *Why*, Izzy?' she said, her face all screwed up. 'What's happened to you, Izzy?'

'What do you care?' I said, becoming angry now. 'You've hardly complained about me going off with Edie. You've been far too busy going clubbing and having a good time with your friends. I'm sure the only reason you brought me here on holiday here was because Mum *made* you.' I knew I was being horrible but I couldn't stop myself.

'That's just not true, Iz,' Ellie said, looking deeply wounded. 'I only seemed happy to let you go off with that Edie girl because I thought that's what *you* wanted. I would've been just as happy spending some time with you.

That's why I wanted you to come out here in the first place – so we could be together.'

A wave of shame washed over me as I tried to blink back the tears.

'Why didn't you tell him you were only sixteen?' she asked. So I explained. And this time I didn't leave anything out.

I poured my heart out to her, telling her about the time Rex and I had first met and the day we spent together on the beach; I told her about the stars and the butterfly and the hippy market, and I showed her my little bracelet that jingled slightly whenever I moved; I explained how much I loved him and that I had never, ever in all my life felt so deeply about another person and that, as far as I was concerned, age was just a number anyway. I told her I was frightened he wouldn't want anything to do with me if I told him the truth, but it had all got so out of hand and before I knew it I had reached the point of no return.

'He needs to know the truth,' she said, after I had finished.

'I will tell him,' I promised, 'and then I can be with him properly.'

'What do you mean, *properly*?' Ellie said, narrowing her eyes suspiciously.

'I'm going to stay here in Ibiza with him – for good,' I said, unquestionably. Suddenly I had never felt so sure about anything in my life before. It was a moment of clarity where everything just clicked into place, and saying it aloud brought with it a soothing calmness.

Despite the confusion and chaos of the past two weeks, one thing was clear above everything: I loved Rex, and, as much as I had to pinch myself to believe it, he loved me too and we had to be together. I realised he might be angry with me for not coming clean about my age from the off but now, after everything, the unbreakable bond I felt we had made, I was sure it would be irrelevant. *It didn't matter how long you'd lived, but* how *you'd lived.* Our love knew no boundaries. Sixteen or sixty, we were so close and in love – and that was what counted.

'Oh don't be so naïve, Izzy,' Ellie scoffed, almost laughing. 'You've obviously looked into the fact that you'll have to travel to the Interior and Justice Central Department in Madrid and provide documentary evidence that you have a source of income before they'll give you a visa and residency, hmm?' I knew she was quoting some kind of bureaucratic legal guff to me, but I didn't care. It was simple to me: I wanted to stay here with him; and I would do whatever it took, even if it meant travelling to Madrid by donkey.

Ellie put her hands up to her head in dismay. 'You know, I never thought something like this would happen. My little sister threatening to run off with a local DJ, who probably does this kind of thing all the time, I should add. I don't suppose you know that in Spain anyone under the age of eighteen is classed as a minor – what do you think he would say if he knew you were a *minor*?' and she overstated the word 'minor' presumably to cause me pain and shame.

'I'm – I'm speechless,' she said. But this was clearly just a figure of speech because she went on . . .

'Think of what you're actually saying, Izzy. I mean, it's just a holiday romance – and one that should never have happened in the first place. It's an infatuation, a fling. You can't make life-changing decisions like that after less than a month of knowing someone. You're only sixteen *and* he doesn't even know your real age!' Ellie's voice was officious and off-hand.

I looked at her, incredulous. How could she think this was all about some stupid crush? She was wrong. Falling in love with Rex had changed my life and the way I thought about *everything*. She might not want to believe it, but I knew it was the truth.

'I thought this holiday would give you and me a chance to be close again, like we once were,' Ellie continued, her voice tinged with regret. 'But now, now you're even more of a stranger to me than before . . .'

Her words stung bitterly. I, too, had hoped that this holiday would give us the chance to talk about stuff as well – not just about Dad, although that would've helped, but just everyday stuff, like friends do, like how we used to. Now, through my lies and deceit, it was worse than ever and I had put even more distance between us.

'I only ever wanted us to be friends, for you to like me and respect me as an adult and not just treat me like your kid sister who gets in the way all the time.' I was wailing now, and Ellie sighed deeply and came towards me and put her arm around me.

'OK. It's OK,' she said resignedly, and I could tell that she was still angry with me but not quite as intensely as before. 'Oh Izzy,' she said, 'You know you can tell me anything. I'm your friend too.'

But it didn't feel like it. There was a gulf the size of an ocean between us – and it was my fault.

'You know you'll have to tell him the truth soon,' she said, handing me a tissue and looking at me pitifully. 'He needs to know.'

And I nodded, because in spite of everything else I knew she was right.

Although Ellie's initial anger at my deception had waned slightly, there was enough of it lingering to make her say that if I didn't call Rex and tell him the truth that afternoon, then she would march down to Café Del Sol tonight and tell him herself. It would be hideous having to tell him face to face, but I figured it would be fifty gazillion times worse if *she* told him. So I called him and he agreed to meet me, and he'd sounded so concerned on the phone that I wondered if I would ever like myself again for putting him, and everyone, through so much worry.

The sun was shining as brightly as ever as I stood outside the lilo shop. I decided that I would ask him to take me to our beach and that we'd walk down to our little alcove, the one where he'd fed me cheese and grapes and nectarines, where we'd shared our first kiss. I would sit him down and take his hand and tell him the truth, right from the start, just as I had done with my sister. I would tell him that I was sorry I had lied to him, but that I thought he would understand and that our love was strong enough to overcome anything.

It was killing me, standing there with the knowledge of what I had to do lingering over me like a great black cloud. I just wanted to get it over with, to blurt it all out and purge myself of it once and for all. I was beginning to get worried. Where was he?

And then I caught sight of his little red moped in the distance and I felt my heart skip a beat, because I knew that I was only minutes away from him holding me tightly in his arms.

I put my hand up to my face to shield my eyes from the sun and watched as he came closer and closer, and I was filled with nerves but still excited at the thought of seeing him again, just like I had been every time we'd met.

He began to wave to signify the fact that he could see me, and I had both my arms in the air and was waving them manically too.

At first I thought I was hallucinating when I saw the van turn the corner and plough into him, the heat finally having got to me. And I didn't really think it was him lying there, bruised and bloodied in the road, just as I had imagined my dad must've looked that time. I was running towards him, even though it didn't feel as though I had any legs and that I was floating like a ghost. I don't remember holding his floppy body in my arms and begging him to breathe and not to die. *Please God, don't let him die. Not Rex. Not like this. I am begging you, just this one thing and*

I will never ask for anything ever again. And I don't remember the ambulance arriving and the paramedics trying to resuscitate him in the road, or the van driver shouting and screaming stuff in Spanish, or the woman who put her arm round me and kept talking to me, even though I couldn't understand what she was saying.

Oddly, I *do* recall getting into the ambulance as it sped off at high speed, and the kind lady paramedic wiping the blood from Rex's nose as I willed him to open those beautiful eyes, those piercing green eyes that had filled me with hope these past couple of weeks. His skin felt warm, which I knew was a good thing. He was damaged, badly damaged, but he was alive. And I thought there must be a God after all.

Chapter 18

Ellie finally made it to the hospital a few hours later. As I saw her, I ran straight into her arms and she hugged me tightly as I broke down and sobbed, my whole body shaking.

'When I heard there'd been an accident, I thought – oh God, I thought it was you! I was so terrified that you'd been hurt, killed, and that it was all because I'd made you go down there and talk to him. My little sister would be dead because of me!' Ellie was ranting and gripping me with such force I could barely catch my breath. 'I love you, Iz, and if anything had happened to you – *anything* – I could never forgive myself.' She was half crying, half laughing, with joy and was kissing me.

'I'm sorry,' was all I managed to say between sobs. 'I'm just so, so sorry.'

The doctors told us that Rex was unconscious, and had shattered his leg and pelvis, and had cracked some ribs. They would need to operate on him. I asked if he would lose his leg and the youngish-looking doctor looked at me kindly and hesitated a bit before saying he didn't know at this stage. I just burst into tears at that because I suddenly had this vision of Rex being confined to a wheelchair for the rest of his life, unable to dive and fish and run along the beach or do any of the things that he loved doing so much and that we all just take for granted.

Once she'd composed herself, Ellie took charge, because that's what Ellie always does in a crisis. She asked why he hadn't come round yet. They said that it was probably due to the shock of the impact, but the fact he'd been wearing his crash helmet had saved his life, and that he was young and strong, and although he wouldn't be playing football anytime soon, he would regain consciousness – and with good rest – he would probably recover in time. Probably. *In time*.

If only I had never lied about my age in the first place then none of this would have happened. Why did good people have to get hurt or die? Was I some kind of jinx?

All this must have brought back hideous memories for Ellie too. Memories of the day our beautiful dad was so cruelly snatched from us in a scarily similar way. I was so grateful Ellie was there, because I knew I couldn't cope on my own. It dawned on me how much she had been a rock in my life – all my life. She had never really failed me. In my selfish way I had resented her for moving on with her life, for trying to come to terms with the past, for having a life that didn't always include me. Really, all she had done was grow up and try to find her own way in this crazy world, just as I was trying to now. I had just been the needy, demanding younger sister, putting pressure on her and emotionally blackmailing her into including me in her life when she had never really excluded me in the first place, and had tried her best this holiday to make me feel part of everything.

I looked at her perfectly familiar face that sometimes, just in a certain turn of the head, reminded me of our dad. Her presence made me realise that for as long as we were both alive we would always have each other and I would never be alone.

A while later, Steve turned up at the hospital. He had heard from the locals that Rex had been involved in an accident, and raced to the hospital as soon as he could. He looked so pale and worried, and I felt for him so much. He smiled a bit when he saw me and we hugged.

'He's going to be OK,' I said weakly, trying to convince myself as much as him.

'I've called his parents,' Steve said. 'They're on their way.'

I nodded and Ellie gave me a reassuring little squeeze.

We weren't allowed to see Rex before he was taken down to the operating theatre, so there was nothing to do other than wait. Wait and hope. So that's what we did.

Steve had gone to get coffee for us all and call Jo-Jo to let her know what had happened, and left me and Ellie sitting on the uncomfortable plastic chairs.

'Don't blame yourself, Iz,' my sister said, as if reading my thoughts. 'You couldn't possibly have known that this would happen.'

'What if he loses his leg, Ellie?' I asked, the words choking me. 'What if something goes wrong on the operating table and he dies? It will be my fault. I should never have hidden the truth from him. I love him,' I whispered. 'I *really* love him, Ellie.'

'I know you do. I know . . .' she said as she stroked my arm, and for the first time I could see that Ellie really did know that this wasn't just some stupid crush.

'All this has reminded me of our dad and that terrible day,' I said, crying even harder now. 'Do you remember, Ellie? Do you think about it too?' I asked, pleading with her.

She was silent for a moment.

'I think about it all the time,' she eventually said, quietly.

'You do?'

'Yes.' Her voice was almost a whisper as she drew breath and began to talk about it. 'I was at ballet class when the police came. I felt so guilty that I wasn't there when they told you. Like I'd let everyone down by not being around to support you,' she said, her pretty face twisting with the pain of the memory. 'After that day, I felt distant from people. Like I was living in a dream – well, more like a nightmare, really. I was terrified of getting too close to anyone: friends, boyfriends – even you and Mum in a way, in case you too were taken away from me.'

I took Ellie's hand but was careful not to say anything. I wanted to let her speak, to finally open up to me, but at the same time I wanted to comfort her, just as she had comforted me. 'It was as if I'd built a wall around my heart, scared to let anyone in. Then Tom came along and – well,' she lowered her eyes and smiled wistfully, 'he broke down those barriers I'd put up, one by one. And gradually I'd stopped being so scared. He helped me come to terms with it all. So you know, Iz, if you do love this guy, it's a good thing. It means that you *can* love. That you've been brave enough to let someone into your heart.' She was crying now and I cried too. I related to her words so much. All along we had felt the same. I just hadn't been able to see it.

She had been hiding her true feelings from me to protect me, putting on a brave front. Perhaps we were not so different after all? Although I didn't want her to be hurting this way, it was a relief to know that she too thought about Dad late at night when it was dark and she couldn't sleep, and that her heart ached when she remembered him, just as mine did, and suddenly I'd never felt closer to her.

Chapter 19

The following day, I met Rex's parents for the first time. They had rushed to the hospital, tired and emotional, straight from the airport and were now in front of Ellie and me in the family waiting area. It was a desolate space with its crude, bare walls and rows of uncomfortable plastic chairs. A coffee vending machine sat sinisterly in the corner, giving out a low, almost inaudible hum, mocking us.

'He phoned me last week,' Rex's mum said, 'and told me he had met someone. I knew you must be special because he never tells me about any girlfriends – and he was right, you *are* beautiful.' She smiled.

I held her hand. It was warming that Rex had mentioned me to her. Usually, I would have been chuffed. But I couldn't allow myself to be, not in the circumstances.

Although the doctors had told us that Rex's operation the previous day had gone well, he would need another to give him the best chance of a full recovery.

'It's quite a tricky procedure,' the doctor had told his parents. 'His bone has been shattered into tiny fragments and we need to try and rebuild the leg back together again, piece by piece, like a jigsaw.'

And so Rex was whisked away again for more surgery, leaving Rex's mum, dad, my sister and me waiting for what seemed like for ever for some news, slumped in the uncomfortable chairs, surrounded by empty polystyrene coffee cups. It was torture, and we didn't really say much because this was hardly the time for small talk.

After what felt like an eternity, a smiley-faced nurse came over and took Rex's parents to one side and I watched them, deep in conversation, and tried to catch the expressions on his parents' concerned faces for any clue as to what she might be telling them. It turned out that Rex's parents were allowed to go in and see him briefly, even though he was still unconscious, and I became euphoric at the thought of seeing him, but the smiley nurse explained that it was family only, and it would be best if I came back tomorrow to see him, because it was getting late. I had wanted to see him so much that I burst into tears again, and Rex's mum put her arm around me and said that it had been a very long day for everyone, and we should all go away and come back in the morning and, hopefully, God willing, Rex would be awake by then. I reluctantly agreed. I had no fight left in me.

The next day, I was allowed in to see Rex. But now that I had permission I was suddenly struck with an overwhelming fear. The man I deeply loved would be lying there unconscious and lifeless. Would I be able to hide my anguish, or would I break down in front of everyone? I had to be a rock for him. I would hold him and be there to comfort him when - and I had to think it would be when, not if - he came round.

The door creaked eerily as I opened it and I saw him, lying there in the cold, clinical hospital bed with his leg in traction, these great horrible pins sticking through a metal cage around his leg as the machines whirred around him.

I was struck by how peaceful he looked. His usually glossy hair was slightly matted on his pillow and his rosebud lips were pink against his skin. Seeing him like that, with tubes stuck all over his perfect body, machines pumping this and that around him and drips feeding him with God only knew what, I almost crumpled to the floor in the crying, sobbing, guilt-wracked mess that I was.

His lips felt warm and dry as I kissed him softly. I saw that one of my tears splashed down on to his cheek. I gently wiped it away. 'I'm so sorry, Rex,' I managed to say. 'I never meant for any of this. I love you. Oh God, I love you so much. I'll never forgive myself if you can't walk again. Please, Rex, wake up . . . Can you hear me, Rex? Please . . .'

I gently lay my head near his chest, careful not to put any pressure on his damaged body, and stayed there until eventually, after what seemed like a lifetime, I fell asleep to the comforting sound of his heartbeat on the monitor.

I had thought of so many things I wanted to say to him, to talk about our future and how I was going to move out to Ibiza. But above all I wanted to tell him the truth about my age, finally, because I needed him to know everything about me. If, like I felt sure he had suggested that night, our future was to be shared, I knew it just didn't matter any more, especially not now. The accident had put everything into perspective for me. The potential fear of losing him had brought it crashing home and made it all so clear. My age was irrelevant in the face of such adversity. All that mattered was that he was alive and that I loved him. And he loved me.

Something woke me with a start and at first I thought it was the whirring sound of the horrible machine that Rex was attached to, but when I looked up he was smiling at me and I could see his eyes, those beautiful deep green eyes that made me want to do cartwheels, were staring straight at me.

'Oh my God, Rex, you're here – you're awake!' I started to cry, but this time they were tears of joy.

'Jeez, what happened?' he croaked, looking a little bewildered.

It felt so befitting that he would regain consciousness while I was there, and I wanted to believe that maybe it had something to do with me; that as much as it had all been my fault, I could be the one to save him, my unyielding love for him strong enough to rouse him from his comatose state.

'How do you feel?' I asked, even though I was frightened of his response.

'Iz,' he said, the fear in his voice cutting through me like a hot knife through butter, 'I can't feel my leg,'

I took his hand in mine and smiled through my tears. 'It's OK, it's just the drugs,' I said soothingly to try and reassure him.

I went and got his parents, because I knew that they would be as happy and overjoyed to see him awake as I was, and that he was going to be OK. I stood at the door as his mum rushed over and held him, cradling his body like a baby, and his dad said that he was so relieved to see him – and everyone was crying, Rex included, so I shut the door and left them to have a private moment together as a family because, for once, I knew it was the right thing to do.

Chapter 20

The apartment looked different somehow. The vibrant laughter and playfulness it had witnessed in the past weeks showed no traces of ever having been there. Now it just felt solemn and desolate, and even the warmth of the sunlight shining through the open patio doors couldn't mask the melancholy that seemed to hang in the air all around us.

No one said anything for a while. We just sat in silence in the soft chairs in the living area of the apartment and it was so quiet you could almost hear everyone's thoughts.

Finally, Narinda said, 'Who wants tea?'

And I smiled sardonically, because it was just such an English thing to say – the man you love lying half dead in a hospital bed? Panic ye not! Have a cup of tea and all will be well! It was like something from a perverse comedy sketch.

'I suppose we should call Mum?' I said as soon as the others left the room, thoughtfully giving Ellie and me some time alone.

Ellie looked up at me and took my hand. Her face was a little puffy from all the recent crying we'd been doing, but it was still perfect in my opinion, even with the absence of make-up.

'I've made a decision,' she said. Her voice was gentle but considered. 'I don't think we should tell her.'

I was shocked. I had just assumed she would want to tell her. After all, it was a pretty big deal.

'You could've been on that bike, Iz. I don't think Mum could cope if she thought you could've been killed in an accident.'

'Do you really think it's best to lie?' I asked. 'You know how Mum has a way of seeing through us.'

'Well, your acting skills must be Oscar standard by now, so maybe she won't guess that something's up,' she said, and I noticed that a small smile was creeping across her face – and it felt so good to see, like a ray of sunshine breaking through the clouds.

I walked to the hospital the next day, bringing with me cheese and grapes and lassi, just as he had done for me that first day we had spent together on the beach. I had found a little bookshop on the way and had gone inside just to have a look and although most of the books were written in Spanish, I found this one little children's book in English entitled *The Cow and the Dog*. It was a story about a cow that had fallen in love with a dog, and everyone had laughed and said 'Cows can't be in love with dogs because one says "Moo" and the other says "Woof".' But the cow felt sure that she was in love with the dog, and eventually it turned out that the dog loved the cow too, and so they stayed together – a cow and a dog, against the odds. It was just the most beautiful story I think I'd ever read and I wrote, *To my darling Rex, you are the dog to my cow. I will love you forever. Moo! Love Iz x* on the inside cover.

When I arrived at the hospital, Rex's parents were sitting with him.

'Hello Izzy, darling,' Daphne said. 'Isn't it marvellous that he's sitting up?'

I beamed at her. 'Yes,' I said, 'it's fantastic.'

'Come on, Bertie,' she said, looking at her husband.

'Sorry, what was that dear?' he replied.

'We'll leave you two to have a catch up,' Daphne said to Rex and me, smiling as she shooed her husband out of the room.

'You look so much better,' I said leaning in to kiss him after they'd gone. 'You look like you again.'

'I'm feeling OK,' he said quietly. 'I'm getting flashbacks of the accident.' He looked distressed. I took his hand in mine and squeezed it reassuringly.

'The doctor says I've probably got post-traumatic stress or something, and that's why I can't quite remember everything. But I'm sure you were upset – there was something you wanted to see me about.'

I knew that now was the time for me to tell the truth. I was apprehensive, yet strangely euphoric at the thought of finally confessing, and adrenaline raced round my system furiously. I drew a deep breath to steady my nerves.

'Yes,' I said. 'You see, I have something to tell you – not that I'm sure it will matter now,' I added, nonchalantly. 'Promise me you won't laugh – or worse, say that you hate me?'

'Izzy,' he said, trying to look at me seriously, 'I could never hate you.'

'Well, I thought so much about what you'd said about a home not being a home unless you have the person you love with you, and I realised that I can't, don't want to be without you. I know that Ibiza is your home and where your heart is, so – well, I've decided that this is where my heart will be too and that I'm going to stay. Come here. To live. With you.'

He stared at me for a few seconds and I was sure I saw tears in his eyes.

'You'd do that for me?' he said. 'Leave your friends and family and your studies to be here, with me?'

'Yes. I *want* to, I so want to.' I smiled at him and he leaned forward slowly as if to kiss me, but I could see that moving caused him a lot of pain, so I leaned in and kissed him softly on the lips.

'I don't know what to say. I mean, I get to keep you! That's almost worth getting run down and nearly killed for!'

'Don't joke,' I said, but I couldn't help smiling too.

'But there's a bit of a problem, you see,' I said. 'Because I'm classed as a minor out here, I'll probably need my mum's written permission before I move and everything. I reckon she'll have kittens when I tell her, but once Ellie, my sister, tells her how much I love you, I know she'll be happy for me, because that's what mums do, right? So I'll go back to London, explain everything, maybe sort out a bit of school stuff first and then come back out as soon as possible.'

Rex stared at me blankly.

'Sorry, Iz,' he said, sounding confused. 'Maybe it's the drugs or something, but you're not making any sense.'

I knew he was right, but I wasn't scared any more. He seemed so ecstatic that I'd said I would move to Ibiza and had looked at me with so much affection that I felt fearless.

'Like I said, please don't laugh or get angry but, well, I didn't quite tell you the whole truth about myself. You see, I'm not really twenty-two. I'm sixteen. I came on holiday with my older sister and *her* friends. I didn't want you to know at first because I thought you wouldn't be interested in me, so I kind of hid the truth from you a little, even though I didn't mean to. And then it just never seemed the right time to tell you. I didn't tell my sister about you either at first but she found out about us and said I had to tell you and then, well, this happened and I . . .'

The expression on Rex's face was beginning to scare me. He looked so shocked I thought he might suddenly slip back into unconsciousness.

'Rex – say something. I'm so sorry I lied, well, more hid the truth than lied,' I said, in a vain attempt to soften the blow, 'but I figured that it doesn't matter any more. We love each other and want to be together – and, well, you said age is just a number, remember?' I said, my voice trailing off at the end.

'You're only sixteen?' he said, his eyes wide with shock.

'Nearly seventeen!' I said brightly, although I could tell this wasn't going exactly as I had hoped and a horrible panic had started to creep into my chest and was squeezing my lungs, making it difficult for me to breathe.

'I had no idea . . . I can't believe you lied to me.' Rex looked at me, confused. 'You're ten years younger than me and you didn't think it would make a difference? And you're here on holiday with your older sister? I – I – can't get my head round this . . .'

He looked hurt and angry and I was scared.

'Please Rex, it doesn't matter now —'

'Doesn't matter?' he said, interrupting me. 'It matters to me . . .'

'I – I thought you wouldn't want to know me if you found out, and well, I just presumed —'

'You presumed wrong,' he said, cutting in sharply. His voice sounded gruff and I passed him some water to sip. He'd been in a coma for three days and now he was getting all distressed because of me and what I'd just told him. I should have picked my moment better, but it couldn't wait any longer – it's not like there is ever a good moment to tell someone you love you've been lying to them.

I looked at him desperately. I could feel myself falling, falling deep down a dark hole with no one there to rescue me.

'You've spun all these lies – made me believe . . . believe you were someone else,' he said. His voice was less gruff, but strained and impassionate.

'But I'm not someone else!' I begged. 'I'm me; I'm Izzy, *your* Izzy. Nothing's changed.'

But I knew it had.

'I think you had better go,' he said with a stoic quietness.

'Please Rex, don't do this,' I begged, and it sounded so undignified, but I didn't care, I had nothing left to lose.

He looked away from me.

'I love you!' I said. 'I really love you and I have meant every word I have ever said to you.'

'Please Izzy, just go,' he said with unfamiliar harshness. 'I need time to think. My head's spinning all over the place. I can't make sense of it all.'

I stood there, my legs threatening to give way beneath me, and I wanted to scream.

I had just been so stupid, so foolish in thinking that he would just shrug his shoulders and say, 'So what? Age is irrelevant when you're in love.' He couldn't even bear to look at me.

I got up to leave, tears streaking my cheeks, and I turned away so he couldn't see my face.

'I got you this,' I said placing the little book, *The Cow and the Dog*, on the edge of the bed. And then I left.

Chapter 21

I cried solidly for two days, two whole days without seeing him, knowing that he was lying there, in a hospital bed after a near-fatal accident, hating me for having lied to him. Ellie had told me I had done the right thing by telling him, but I had said that if that was the case then why did it hurt so much? She couldn't really answer me, which had made me feel even worse. On top of everything, we were due to go home tomorrow.

Ellie was right, I had been so naïve. Age wasn't just a number – it *had* mattered to him, the fact I was so much younger.

I thought back to the conversation we'd had at his villa when we had talked about the future, our future together, and he'd hinted at settling down. There had been that moment of doubt, a flicker of fear that we might want different things at different times because of the whole age gap thing. I had tried to gloss over it, to pretend it wasn't an issue, but a small part of me had been concerned. Would I be ready for marriage and children by the time he wanted them? Would I have experienced the things in life I hoped I would before that happened? I had felt sure we could overcome any potential problems together, though – our love for each other conquering all.

I wondered if he now regretted having said all those

amazing things that he had said to me, like how special I was and how he loved me. Did he want to take it all back now that he knew the truth? Had it really changed everything?

I wondered what Rex had told his parents and Steve and Jo-Jo. They would ask why I hadn't been at the hospital, and I felt a stabbing pain in my chest as I imagined their jaws dropping as he told them what a liar I was and that he never wanted to see me again. I was so ashamed of myself. By not being brave enough to be honest, I had hurt the person I loved more than anyone. I felt so sorry for myself, because I should have known that this would happen – that I, Izzy Jackson, was just such a loser, because even when something amazing like meeting Rex happened to me, I had spectacularly blown it. And then I hated myself even more for feeling sorry for myself because I wasn't the one lying in a hospital bed who might never walk again. I wondered if it was possible to die from hating yourself so intensely, because I felt sure that if it was I would drop down dead that very minute.

It was no good. I had to see him before we left. I had to try and make him understand. Beg and plead for his forgiveness. He would see how much I really did love him and it would be enough to cast aside his doubts. He would welcome me back into his arms and hold me and tell me that despite everything, the lying and the age difference, he knew in his heart that I was 'the one' and that we would get there, just like the cow and the dog, against the odds.

I walked to the hospital. I felt that I needed to be alone and that maybe this would be my last chance to breathe in the

Ibizan air that had been so fragrantly sweet and full of promise these last three weeks. Soon I would be on a plane home and I might never get the chance to see the beach again, to watch the waves gently wash against the soft sand and the pine trees swaying in the warm breeze. A small part of me was hopeful he would change his mind and forgive me and ask me to stay. I imagined him holding my hand in his and telling me that he couldn't imagine his life without me in it, just like I couldn't imagine my life without him, and the world would once again feel as though it belonged only to us.

I walked along the dusty road and past the lush olive groves and orange trees, their branches heavy with fruit, and the small café where we'd drunk lattes and strawberry lassis, and it was silent but for the jingle of the little bells on my bracelet.

It was close to sunset by the time I reached the hospital, and I was relieved when I saw that Rex's family wasn't around. The nurse led me through the white swinging doors and I saw the familiar uncomfortable chairs that I had spent so long sitting on during the last few days. I knocked on the door.

'I knew it would be you,' he said as I entered. His tone was soft and more like it used to be. Instantly I felt more at ease. 'I'm glad you came.'

I wanted to kiss him, but was frightened he would reject me. I knew I wouldn't be able to cope with that so I resisted.

'You are?' I asked, hopefully.

'Yes, I am,' he said, and he smiled at me and held his arms out. I ran into them and he made a little 'oof' noise as if I had hurt him, so I relaxed a little and just stayed there, breathing in the scent of him deeply.

'I thought you hated me and never wanted to see me again,' I said, resting my head underneath his chin.

'I told you,' he said, 'I could never hate you, Izzy. I was just, well, shocked by your confession. It's a lot to take in . . .'

'I know, I'm sorry,' I said, looking up at him now. 'Please forgive me. I'm a fool. I was just so scared of losing you. I've never met anyone like you before and I couldn't believe it when you seemed genuinely interested in me. I knew, well, I thought that if you knew I was that much younger, then you just wouldn't want to know me.'

He smiled, but it was one of those smiles that you know people only give to make you feel better and I could feel the floor drop from beneath me.

He sighed ruefully, as he stroked my hair. I started to cry again, those wretched tears, and he brushed them away, every single one that fell from my eyes.

I sensed I was losing him. I was watching him slip away before my very eyes and deep down I knew there was nothing I could do. But I had to try. I couldn't give up on him, on us . . .

'I still want to come out here to live, to be with you,' I said, desperately. 'I figure as long as I do well in my studies and everything, Mum'll give me her blessing and maybe even be happy for me and . . .'

I looked at him. His eyes seemed darker somehow, the brightness in them dull and distant. My world was falling apart at the seams like my nan's old vintage bag which had burst in front of him that time. 'I'm sorry, Iz,' he interrupted me gently. 'It can't happen.'

'But you know everything now. No more secrets, I promise,' I said, the panic engulfing me, carrying me away, kicking and screaming, to another place where Rex and I didn't exist.

'I almost lost my leg and I'm going to be laid up in this hospital bed for months,' he sighed. 'The doctors reckon, if I'm lucky, I could be out around Christmas time, and then I'll have to have months and months of physiotherapy to help me walk again, if I ever do . . .'

I saw a sorrow in him that I'd never seen before. It wasn't one of self-pity, more of resignation to a reality that he knew I couldn't be part of.

'You will!' I cried, not wanting to hear him say stuff like that.

'Well maybe, but it's going to be a long, slow and probably painful process. My leg is being held together with more metal than a cutlery factory.' He laughed a little, but I couldn't bring myself to. 'I'll need to be in a wheelchair for a while – they can't say for how long – and maybe, if I do manage to learn to walk properly again, I will need a stick, probably for the rest of my life. I'll have a limp,' he said coldly, although I could tell that really, like me, he was terrified. 'I'll be an invalid, Iz,' he said, his voice wavering now. 'I'll never be able to dive again like I used to, or run down the beach and dance on tables, or ride my moped or —'

I couldn't bear to hear any more. 'Stop! Of course you'll be able to do those things,' I told him, 'and even better than before.'

'Oh, Iz,' he said, looking at me. He looked so bereft, as if seeing the pain in my eyes hurt him as much as it did me. 'I'm not lying. It's what they've told me. It's the truth. I have to accept it and so do you. You can't come out here, not now. You have your whole life ahead of you. You mustn't give your life up to look after a cripple who'll need help washing himself and getting dressed in the mornings.' The harshness of his words wrapped around my throat and choked me. 'You're so young, and I don't mean to sound patronising, but it's a fact, just as this is,' he said, pointing to his leg. 'So you have to go home and get on with your life; achieve all the things you want to do, become a vet, swim with dolphins, see your friends, go clubbing – normal stuff.'

'I don't want any of that,' I almost screamed. 'It all means nothing without you!' I was so desperate I wanted to pound the walls with my fists. I was losing him and the pain of knowing this ripped into my soul and tore it apart. He was trying to set me free. But I didn't want to be free. I was content to remain captured by his love for ever, whatever hardship that meant for both of us.

He shook his head forlornly. 'My mum is going to come out here. She's going to take care of me, like I'm five years old again or something,' he said, with a helplessness that destroyed me further. 'I can't let you give up your life for me. I won't let you do it, even if you could.'

'Would it make any difference if I really was twenty-two?' I asked, frantically searching for a drop of hope as the walls started to close in around me, making me feel claustrophobic.

But he didn't answer. He just shook his head sadly as he took my hand in his. 'Please don't cry. Be strong. Be brave, because you know, you're one of the bravest women I've ever met. I admired your courage so much when you opened up to me that time on the beach. It's a lot for a young –' and he paused again, '– a lot for anyone to deal with.'

I knew he had made up his mind. We would never get to live our Ibiza dream, not now, not ever. I would go home and he would still be here and there would just be memories – memories that would fade in time like an old photograph that has been left in the sun. They would gradually slip away, the years making them all fuzzy and distorted and I knew, right in that moment, that nothing in my life would ever be the same again.

Chapter 22

I t was stuffy and hot as we headed towards the airport in a taxi, and no one spoke. We were all too wrapped up in our own private thoughts for chit-chat.

Saying goodbye to Rex had been the hardest thing I had ever had to do, next to burying my dad. I didn't want to imagine a life without Rex. He had switched the lights on in my heart, in my soul. Since I had found him, I had seen the world in vibrant colour for the first time. And now it would be dark again and I would be alone.

He had kissed me so tenderly before I left, and even though I knew it would be our last ever kiss and that my heart would never miss a beat in the same way again like it did with him, I told myself that this was not really goodbye and that somehow fate would intervene and throw us back into each other's arms just as it had brought us together. I knew I was kidding myself like I always did, but I needed to protect myself from the stark reality of it; the cold, dreaded truth that had hurt so much and continued to hurt me now. He had held me in his arms and it had felt like he would never let go, our hearts and spirits forever intertwined with our bodies. I had suddenly been aware of the fact that I would never have this feeling again. It would never be the same with anyone else. The little in-jokes that we had that made us laugh; the conversations we'd had that had brought us close together and strengthened our love.

Eventually, he had loosened his grip on me in his arms and said it was getting late and that he was worried about me walking home in the dark. But I wasn't scared; somehow the night gave me a kind of comfort, a warm, dark blanket wrapping itself around me, sheltering me from the agony of leaving him and hiding my pain. I had looked at him for what I knew was the last time I probably ever would and I said, 'I love you, Rex Brown.' That's all there really was left to say in the end. Yet somehow, saying it didn't nearly explain the regret and sense of loss I was feeling or how much I really did love him, and I wished I could think of bigger, better words.

I had picked up my little rucksack and turned to look at him, just one last glance. He looked so beautiful, almost like a memory fading in front of my very eyes. I realised that I didn't even have a photograph of him. Not one. We had been far too caught up in the moments we'd shared, too busy falling in love to even think of such things. But now it seemed like an oversight. I had nothing to hold or look at and remind me of him when my memory would inevitably begin to fail me. I suddenly panicked, another layer of despair adding to my prospering pain, because when I tried to picture his face I found that I couldn't visualise all the little details: the way his eyes shone like emeralds as they caught the light, or how he always seemed to cock his head to one side whenever he asked a question; and the harder I tried, the more unclear the image of him became, and I squeezed my eyes together in a desperate attempt to clear my brain.

The queue to check in was long and full of our fellow holiday-makers returning home, back to their everyday lives and whatever they might hold. I watched as I saw gangs of girls and lads who had just arrived in Ibiza, looking pale and excited at the prospect of what a few weeks on this amazing island would hold for them, just as we had been three weeks ago. I was envious of their anticipation, of the delights they would encounter and how these would take them to places they never knew existed in their minds. Maybe they too would fall in love? I was sure of one thing: they would never feel the same after their Ibiza experience. Rex had been right. There was something about the island that was a little bit magic.

I decided to go outside for a bit of fresh air. Ellie had said that this was fine – I think she understood that I needed to be alone, to think and work things out in my head. So I walked through the electric sliding doors and found a grass verge just outside the airport that was out of the way of all the holiday-makers, and smokers madly chuffing away on their last cigarette before they boarded their flight, and I slumped down.

The sun was scorching and I loosened the ties of my strappy top that was digging into my neck slightly and pulled my knees up to my chest. I had experienced so many emotions these past few weeks: happiness, sadness, fear, rejection, relief, and guilt – right through the spectrum, and I suddenly felt exhausted. Above all though, I realised I had connected with someone like I had never done before and that it had taken me on a journey that was so much more than I could ever have imagined. I had discovered part of myself that I didn't know existed, a part of me that could love another human being with such passion and intensity that it made my head swim and my heart swell – and it had felt so good, so unbelievably good, and I knew that this was also the reason I felt so bad. Wherever there is up, it seems there is also down, and the higher you travel the further it is to come back to earth. I wondered when the pain would stop. Would I one day wake up and be free of it? Or would it be a pain that would gradually fade away, like the sea washes away the names of two people in love written in the sand?

And as I was thinking this, I saw something out of the corner of my eye. No, it couldn't be, could it? But it was. A beautiful little butterfly had landed on my right knee, just as it had done that time with Rex on the beach. I gasped loudly because it was just so strange and coincidental, and I looked around for someone, anyone, who could witness this mini miracle, because I swore no one would have ever believed it. I could hardly believe it myself. It was somehow fitting, though, like a final message sent to me from Rex, from my dad, from whoever it was that was watching over me, because I felt sure that someone had to be. I was convinced it was looking at me, this tiny little butterfly, with its vibrant, iridescent wings and its antennae twitching, telling me that everything would be OK and that I was safe and loved and that I would be happy again some day, despite the pain I felt now. I stared at the small creature, which was now blurred through my tears, and wondered if in fact everything in life goes full circle and that whatever journey you take you always come right back to the place that you started and everything begins again. And it gave me peace, that little butterfly, a moment of peace as my heart was breaking.

Epilogue

As I sat on the plane, watching everyone cram their bags of duty free into the overhead lockers and fight over the window seat, I once again found myself thinking of home. In spite of everything, it was strangely reassuring to know that in a couple of hours' time Greg would be picking us up from the airport and Mum would be waiting for us at home, no doubt having cooked something yummy like her special homemade lasagne. I would stroke Montague, and call Willow and hope that things would be OK between us – and even if she had found a new friend, perhaps it would be all right and we could all be friends and hang out together. I realised now that nothing ever stays the same and that things must change and move on.

A man over the loudspeaker said, 'Ladies and gentlemen, welcome aboard flight BK347 to London Heathrow. Please ensure all electronic equipment and mobile phones are switched off for the duration of the flight . . .' and I remembered that I still had my mobile on, so I reached inside my bag to get it. I saw that there was a text message and I presumed it must be from Wils because no one else ever texted me. But it wasn't.

LOOK INSIDE YOUR BAG. LOVE R X

I felt my heart flip in my chest and frantically began

fumbling inside my rucksack for whatever it was that he might be referring to, but all I could find was my old junk: some socks to keep my feet warm on the flight and an old copy of *Gloss* magazine I'd bought on the way here. But then I unzipped the little secret pocket. Inside was an envelope.

My dearest Isabelle,

I'm writing this from my sick bed, so please excuse the bad handwriting as it's not the easiest thing to write with your left leg sticking up in the air.

It's a beautiful day outside. I can see from my window that the sun is shining and there's a gentle breeze – just the right sort of weather for a trip to Cala Jondal. Only I don't know if I'll ever be able to go there again. Not because of the leg or anything, but because it will always remind me of you – of us and the times we spent there together – and I know that if I do ever go back, it will never feel the same. Please don't be sad, Iz. The last three weeks have been too amazing for sadness, wouldn't you agree? As you might say, it would be 'churlish' to think otherwise (and I don't mean that in a facetious way! Ha ha!).

You are one of the most special people, if not the most special person, I have ever met in my life (and remember I've been around a bit longer than you, not being funny or anything) and it has been a privilege to have spent this time with you. Although some might say that three weeks is no time at all, to me it has felt like a precious lifetime.

I realise now that you were meant to come into my life for a reason; to show me what it feels like to love and be loved, and for that I will always thank you.

Don't beat yourself up over the whole age thing, although I know you will. What matters is that we found each other and, although the heart is deceitful above all things, I know that you are a decent and honest woman and will someday make the most amazing wife and mother. I truly envy that guy.

To me you will always be like that butterfly on the beach, a beautiful butterfly that flew into my life and enchanted me and then flew away again. This is how it was supposed to be.

I'll never forget you, Isabelle Jackson, and neither will Ibiza. Just like this amazing island ,you captured my heart and will forever be a part of me.

Be safe, be happy, but above all, be you, because you are beautiful, inside and out.

I have enclosed some things I think you should have. I don't need them any more. For me, the memories will always be enough.

Promise me that one day you'll swim with the dolphins.

Goodbye first. Woof Woof.

Love,
Rex x

And inside the envelope were the beads that Juan Pablo had given him and a shell that I presumed could only be from our beach, one that he had used to write the giant 'I love you Isabelle' in the sand, and I clutched them to my chest tightly.

I noticed that he'd written something in small handwriting at the bottom of the letter.

P.S. If you're still wondering how I knew your name that first time we met, check your photo wallet.

I frantically located the little black photo wallet in my bag and stared at it for ages in the vain hope that some kind of clue would leap out at me, but I couldn't see anything other than photos: one of me and Wils taken at her sixteenth birthday party, a couple of Montague and me at home, one of Ellie with Mum – Ellie looking her usual glamorous self . . . I went through the wallet twice, but there was nothing. I was about to give up, then something caught my eye. On the back of the wallet, among the many stickers and pictures of Wils and me, was this faded photograph of me and my dad – you know, one of those sticker-type ones you have taken in a booth where you can choose a funny frame – and underneath I had written, *Isabelle (aged ten) and her daddy xxx*. It was one of the last photographs ever taken of my dad and me, and I had completely forgotten it was there. Rex must've seen it that time my vintage bag had exploded in front of him at Alfredo's party, and guessed it must be me in the picture.

I smiled as I stared at that tiny picture; I looked so young, with a chubby face and wide eyes, and my dad looked so wonderful and strong and loving, and we both looked so happy, neither of us knowing what the future held for us, just living in that moment in time. And I thought how much Rex and my dad had in common in a strange way, because I knew he'd been right all along: just because someone isn't there any more, doesn't mean that we will ever stop loving them.